Snowed
in at
Shenandoah Valley

a novel

TINA MARTIN

Acknowledgements

I am truly grateful for the readers who've been traveling with me throughout this writing journey. Y'all know I like to mix it up, but I always keep it real. I strive for originality in everything I do, and y'all just roll right along with it. I love the enthusiasm! I'm thankful for your awareness that writing is creativity. It's art. It's what I love to do and therefore, I'll keep doing it as artfully as I can.

I couldn't do this without my beta team, my editor and proofreaders and everyone else who offer input into this process. I'm forever thankful for the love and support of my family.

TINA MARTIN

SNOWED IN AT *Shenandoah Valley*

Snowed
in at
Shenandoah Valley

SNOWED IN AT *Shenandoah Valley*

CHAPTER 1

"I CAN'T BELIEVE you got me out here in these streets like this, Sariah!" Deja Barnett said aloud with the windshield wipers on the highest setting to prevent snowflakes from obstructing her view on the three-lane, crowded highway. Her hands gripped the steering wheel like they were duct-taped to it and, for some reason, the heat had conked out ten miles back, blowing cold, bone-chilling air. Or, perhaps, it was just *that* cold outside, making the heat inside struggle to work. The heat said, 'girl, bye' and left Deja to fend for herself like Sariah had done — left her. Left her with all of *her* wedding preparations.

That's why Deja was on the road. She was heading to Shenandoah Valley to handle some key wedding arrangements for her sister — the type of things Deja thought the bride would insist on handling firsthand, especially a bride as meticulous as Sariah. Sariah wanted her wedding to go off without a hitch but was too busy to make the trip to the valley. As the maid of honor, it was Deja's obligatory duty to perform such *menial* tasks, but nothing Deja would do was menial. Those were Sariah's words: *menial tasks*. It was like Sariah was the CEO of her wedding and Deja was her underpaid, overworked administrative assistant who fetched coffee, or in this case, ate cake. Sariah took the *maid* in maid of honor a little *too* literal.

In fulfilling her obligations, Deja found herself in the midst of a snow shower, a sea of red brake lights and beeping horns on 81 North. The majestic mountains stood tall above the chaos below, showing off their beauty that Deja could fully take in now since traffic wasn't moving. The snowcaps on them added to their splendor, but in Deja's world, all this beauty was meant to be enjoyed from indoors with a cup of hot chocolate, a pair of thick socks and a toasty fire or at least some working central heat. Being stuck in a cocoon on an Interstate, in a snowstorm with faulty heat was not a good look.

Completely agitated, she slapped the horn as if its dainty, little beep would encourage the movement of the standstill traffic and yelled, "Come on! What's the holdup?" But, just like her love life, traffic was going nowhere fast.

Inching along at five snail-miles per hour, she asked herself why her sister had to get married in the dead of winter at the Blue Ridge Mountains. Most people preferred spring, summer or autumn weddings. Sariah Barnett – she *had* to have a frostbite wedding. In January. The second coldest month in the United States, often confused with the first coldest. Had she known Sariah wanted to have a winter wedding, she'd let her choose one of her boujee friends to be her maid of honor. But it was too late now. She was in the thick of it – in the *thick* of the snow, in the *thick* of this trip, the traffic – in the *thick* of it all.

"Uh, come on people…" Deja said. She was going nowhere fast and still had another fifteen miles before her exit. She'd turned the radio down since it had started snowing because everybody and they mama were under the false assumption that you could *drive* better and *see* better without all the noise, but since it was her only form of entertainment at the moment and her *only* distraction from traffic, she considered turning it back up.

She crept along further. "Ooh, Sariah, you owe me big time for this," she grumbled. "Big time! I can't believe this. Urghhhh!"

In the left lane, the 'fast' lane (but nothing about it was *fast* today) she observed a four-car pileup. Creeping further along, she noticed cars on the shoulder. Somebody's grandma had pulled over to wait until the snow stopped and other people followed suit, deciding it was a good idea.

Deja blew back a ringlet of hair that bounced down to her forehead. She wasn't waiting for a thing! She had places to go. People to see. Cake to taste. She couldn't do that sitting beside the road, suffering defeat by the white stuff falling from the sky. Besides, she wanted to get to Shenandoah Valley before nightfall, but at this rate, who knew when she'd arrive?

The red lights were still plentiful. People were honking horns, getting agitated with all the stop-and-go traffic. Some drivers insisted on changing lanes like that would solve their problems. Deja glanced through her rearview mirror and saw an eighteen-wheeler behind her. Looming. Stalking. She always thought tractor-trailers looked *mean* as if you could attach an emotion to a vehicle. This one was red with orange marker lights lined all around its frame, making it easier for other drivers to see it in the dark, but it also gave it a little personality, too – one that made her nervous.

Deja glanced in the mirror again. She didn't feel comfortable with the truck behind her. She thought about switching lanes, but one wrong move and she'd be squished like an accordion – like the two cars in the middle of the four-car accident she'd passed. "Ugh…stop looking in the mirror and drive," she told herself, her breath hovering in front of her mouth. That's how cold it was in her car.

She turned the radio off and refocused her attention on the road. Up ahead she could see blue lights from multiple police cruisers. The traffic appeared to be moving along a little better after she passed them.

"Finally!" she said, relieved.

Things were looking up – that is until her car started making strange noises – noise she had never heard before. Noise that made her heart pound against her rib cage.

Grum, grum, grum. Blub, blub, blu, blu, blu, bluuuuuuuuub!

"What in the world?"

Deja looked at the temperature gauge on the dash. The meter laid all the way over to the red side. She didn't know much about cars, but she knew the temperature gauge needle was supposed to be in the middle.

"Great! Just freakin' great!"

She had to *blub, blub, blub* her way over to the shoulder now. She glanced in the rearview mirror. Mean truck was still there but kept its distance as she moved over to the slow lane. The roads were slick. The snow, relentless. Pulling over to the shoulder proved to be a challenge. She needed to get as far off of the road as possible without sliding into the guardrail. Slowly and methodically, she made the transition, feeling the wheels sliding beneath her. She tried not to freak out in the process, but as a North Carolinian, she wasn't used to this.

"Whew! I made it!"

She shut off the car. That's when she saw steam rising from the hood. Or was that smoke?

"Now what are you going to do, Deja?"

She snatched her cell phone from the passenger seat and angry-dialed her sister.

Sariah answered, "Are you there yet, Dej?"

"No, I'm not *there yet*. I'm—"

"Jeez Louise," Sariah said, cutting her off. "You drive slower than the line moves at the DMV."

"I'm *not* driving. That's the problem. Do you know where I am right now, Sariah? No, you don't, so let me tell you. I'm beside the road, *stuck* in a friggin' snowstorm, and not only am I *stuck*, but my car went up in smoke!"

Sariah giggled. "Deja, stop being so doggone dramatic."

"I'm not being dramatic. Smoke is pouring from the hood of my car. Now, I'm stranded."

"Ugh. Don't you ever do any maintenance on that metal pill bottle you call a car?"

"If by maintenance you mean getting my oil changed, yes!" Deja said. Besides getting new tires, that's all the maintenance single women usually did on their vehicles.

Sariah snickered. "Oil change, Deja? That's it?"

"Yeah! How do you think I made it this far?"

"Jesus."

Deja's jaw clenched. "I don't even know why I called you. You'd rather berate me than help."

"How am I supposed to help? I have no idea where you are."

"I'm like an hour away from the valley, but I'm

stuck now. I'm stranded on the highway! This is a woman's worst nightmare!"

"*Puh-leese*. Gaining a pound is my worst nightmare. What you're experiencing is an adventure."

"An adventure?"

"Yes, and before you hyperventilate, just call a tow."

"A tow! Are you kidding me?"

"Deja, don't you have roadside service? That's why they exist."

Annoyed by her sister's nonchalance, she said, "See, that's why I should've let you do this yourself! After all, it is your *fabulous* wedding."

"I didn't have time to do it, Deja. I'm tied up with other things. You'll understand one day when you *actually* start dating. And while we're on the subject, when will that be, Deja? I'm tired of mom asking me if you're seeing somebody. What's your problem with guys?"

"I don't have a problem! I—"

Glancing at the side-view mirror, Deja paused when she saw a GMC pickup truck pull up behind her.

"Hell-oooooooo?" Sariah sang into the receiver.

"We'll finish this later. I gotta go." She ended the call but held on to her cell phone as she watched a man get out of the truck wearing a black peacoat, a black and white winter scarf and a red toboggan. Now, he was walking toward her car.

"Oh, no. This ain't going to go well…" Deja said. She wasn't exactly what you would call a people-person, and she understood that about herself, but other folk did not. They assumed she had a few screws loose and let her be.

Now, some man was walking up on her. She assumed he was in law enforcement. Ordinary people didn't stop for stranded motorists these days, did they?

He tapped on her window with a gloved hand. She rolled the window down to a paper-thin crack and asked, "Can I help you, officer?" Her breath fogged the window.

He smiled.

Deja noticed his teeth were whiter than the beautiful snowflakes landing on his beard, coat and hat. *Wow*, she thought, instantly feeling a rush of blood to her brain. He was bundled for the elements, but she could still tell he had it going on.

He said, "I'm not an officer, ma'am. I saw your car steaming. I figured I'd pull over to lend you a hand."

"Oh, um, that's nice of you and all, but I'm good, officer."

He narrowed his gaze at the lady. He'd already told her he wasn't an officer, yet she was still referring to him as one. Was she that nervous? He looked at the hood, smelled coolant and said, "You're not good. I think your engine overheated. There's no way you can drive it any further."

"Oh, uh, well, that's a bummer, isn't it? Anyway, thanks for stopping by." Deja rolled the window back up, but the man was still standing there. Using his knuckles, he tapped on the glass again.

Deja inched the window down to an even smaller crack than before. "Yes?"

"I can pull your car to the next exit. At least, that way, it'll be off of the freeway."

Why is he so eager to help me? Seems suspect…

"I appreciate the offer, but I'm good," Deja told the eager man. "I have roadside service."

"With this traffic and the storm, roadside service probably won't be here for a few hours yet."

She chewed her lip. The tall, well-spoken stranger with flawless teeth was right, but what was she supposed to do? Get into a car with a complete stranger? Then she thought about those people who freely summoned a lift on those rideshare apps. They rode with strangers all the time and that was to get rides after a night of drinking and partying. Being stranded in a snowstorm was no party. This was an extreme circumstance. She could freeze her behind off beside the road or get rammed by a car or tractor-trailer skidding out of control. She had to do something. Besides, he seemed nice enough.

She sighed and said, "Um, okay, but just off

the freeway and then we go our separate ways."

"Yes, ma'am."

He walked back to his truck and when he had clearance, he pulled out onto the street, passed her car and pulled over again. He backed up the truck until it was close enough to hook up her car to it. After he had accomplished the task, he walked back to her car and said, "Shift the gear to neutral."

"Okay," she said, doing as he asked.

He said, "Okay, you can get out now."

She grimaced. That wasn't a part of the plan. "What?"

"You can get out now. You know you have to ride with me, right?"

"I can't sit here and steer while you pull me?" she asked, trying to come up with a scenario where she didn't have to be enclosed in a vehicle with him.

He grinned again. "No, ma'am. There would be no reason to steer if I'm pulling the car."

"Oh. Right. Well, what if I don't touch the wheel?"

"That's not safe. Come on. You'll be fine in the truck with me. I'm harmless."

Perhaps the last words she'd hear before being bludgeoned to death…

"Okay," she said, grabbing her purse. She stepped out of the car. Snowflakes dwindled, landing delicately on her brown ringlets. Her flats were no match for the snow and ice. She was falling backward when he caught her.

"Whew! That was close. Thank you," she said, looking up at him. Snowflakes showered them both.

"No problem."

She found herself impressed by his willingness to help and quite taken by the way he towered over her like the mountains. And he looked just as royal.

Lofty.

Distinguished.

Dignified.

Striking.

She was five-feet-six, so she could appreciate a tall, statuesque man, especially one as attractive as him – one she was instantly drawn to.

He found himself impressed as well. He'd been enchanted by her cocoa-colored skin and how the wind-tossed her brown, shoulder-length curls. Temptation wreaked havoc on his fingers, urging him to brush the snow off of her gorgeous strands, but he just stood there in awe of how that luscious hair framed such a pretty face. Those high cheekbones elevated her from pretty to utterly beautiful. Her full, gloss pink-tinted lips caught his attention, but so did her brilliant, golden-brown eyes. Where did the beauty end for this woman? The answer: it didn't. Everything about her was enough to take any man's breath.

He pushed those thoughts aside and took a closer look at her shoes. He noticed they were dressy shoes, and she didn't have any socks, stockings — anything. She may as well had gone barefoot. And she didn't have a hat to cover all that pretty brown hair of hers. Was she not aware of the weather as she planned her travels? She couldn't have been. She was nowhere near dressed appropriately for winter.

Holding her arm to help her maintain her balance, he opened the door to his truck, assisted her with getting inside and then walked around the front to get on the driver's side. After securing his seatbelt, he shifted the truck into the drive position and said, "At this rate, we should get to that exit in about twenty minutes or so."

"Okay." Deja held on tight to her purse, overwhelmed by the masculine energy in her new surroundings. The entire truck smelled like a man — earthy and woodsy like incense and sandalwood with a hint of leather. With the hat on, she couldn't make out much of his features, but she knew he was devilishly handsome. Nice lips. A stately nose. Light-complexioned skin tone. His thick beard made him ten times more desirable than a man without one. And there was something else about him…something she couldn't quite put her finger on. Maybe it was just the feeling of being with him. A vibe. A sense of calmness that told her, even though she was with a stranger, she knew she'd be okay.

She glanced over at him again. He was driving, checking the mirror occasionally to make sure the car was okay. He gave her a quick glance when he felt her staring at him. She hurriedly looked away to avoid any prolonged eye contact.

"I saw you had North Carolina plates. Whereabout in NC are you from?" he asked.

"Chapel Hill," she answered, remembering she'd crossed over into Virginia a little over three hours ago.

"Is that near anywhere near Durham?"

"Yeah, it is!" Deja said, probably a little more excited than she needed to be. Than she *wanted* to be. "Durham is like Chapel Hill's big brother."

"Is that right?" he asked.

"Yes. Where are you from?"

A patch of snow flew off the car in front of him and landed on his windshield.

"Whoa! Where'd that come from?" Deja asked.

"It came from the roof of the car in front of me. That's why it's so important to clean all the snow off your car before hitting the road. It can cause an accident."

"I see."

He increased the speed of the wipers to clear the windshield, then said, "You asked me a question."

"Oh, yeah. Where are you from?"

"I live in Harrisonburg."

"Harrisonburg. Never heard of it. Is that in Virginia or North Carolina?"

"Virginia." He glanced over at her and asked,

"What brings you to this neck of the woods?"

"My sister. She's getting married in the valley and wants me to check out the venue, attend the cake tasting—anything she can think of to make her special day flawless, I'm responsible for doing it."

"Wow. She must really trust you."

"It's not about trust. She just doesn't want to be bothered with any of it."

"But it's her wedding."

"Exactly. You get it. Finally! Somebody gets it!" *I only had to travel to another state for somebody to see my view.*

"Have you expressed to her that you don't feel comfortable handling those tasks?"

"Yes, I have, but yet, here I am. I mean, honestly, how am I supposed to know if the cake is to her liking? I swear she doesn't want to do the tasting because she's afraid one bite is going to tip the scale. She already weighs absolutely nothing, and when I say nothing, I'm talking *air*. And don't get me started on that fiancé of hers. Ugh…he's a stuck up lil' weasel of a jerk."

The man chuckled, checking the mirrors again. "Is that right?"

"Sure is. You know how people get this stale look on their faces when they know they've done something wrong? That's how this clown looks all the time. He always looks guilty like a car salesman trying to sell a single mother a lemon when he *knows* it's a lemon. I can't stand him. I don't even know how my sister does. Oh, wait—I know. She's never around him! I can count on one hand how many times I've seen them together in the last year."

"That's because you purposely stay away given your dislike of him."

"I doubt it," she replied. "Why would you marry somebody you don't like to be around?"

"Some people get married for status, I suppose."

"That's insane."

"It's also insane for you to be up here handling all of your sister's wedding affairs, but you're here, aren't you?"

"Against my will. Yes."

She digressed and checked her phone. She saw a missed call from Sariah, followed by a text:

Why'd you hang up on me??

"Pardon me, but I didn't catch your name," the man said.

She dropped the frown from her forehead and decided not to respond to Sariah. Looking over at the man, she said, "Oh, how rude. I'm Deja."

"Your name is Deja?"

"Yeah, like déjà vu. I get that all the time. Go ahead. Laugh it up."

"I wasn't going to laugh. I think it's unique."

"Mmm-hmm…and what's your name?" she asked.

"Dare."

"You said Dare?"

"Yep."

"As in, I *dare* you to run barefoot in the snow. That dare?"

He chuckled. "Yes, and it's spelled like that as well."

"Nice."

After a few more minutes of driving, they finally reached the exit. Dare pulled over on the shoulder and said, "So, what's your end game?"

"For what? The wedding?"

"No. For now. I towed your car off the freeway. Now what?"

Deja took in the snowy landscape, rubbed her hands together and said, "I'll sit in my car and wait for roadside service to show up."

"That could take hours."

"I'll be fine."

"I don't think so. What kind of man would I be if I left you stranded in the snow beside the road with no heat?"

"Well, you've done quite enough for me already, Dare. I don't want to put you out."

"Nonsense. How about I tow you to your hotel or wherever you're staying? Where are you staying, anyway?"

"At the Massanutten Resort. That's where my sister is getting married."

"Then I'll tow your car there. It'll be convenient for you to be in the warmth and comfort of your condo while roadside service makes the necessary repairs to your car."

"Yeah, but—"

"I'm not taking no for an answer, Deja. I can't. It's not in my nature to leave you stranded like this."

Dang.

Deja beamed with appreciation. Dare had a nurturing, protective side she adored. A man like him had to be taken, she surmised, but she couldn't tell if he was wearing a ring beneath the thick gloves he had on. Even if he wasn't, she was sure he had a girlfriend.

"Then I guess it's settled," she said, caving to his request.

He gave her a single nod before shifting the truck back into gear. He checked the mirrors and safely merged back onto the road.

"Do you know how far the resort is from here?" Deja inquired.

"About thirty minutes, give or take. That's not bad, right?"

"No, it's not. I feel like I've been on the road forever."

"That's because of this traffic. There are accidents all over the place. The best and safest place to be right now is indoors."

"With some heat," she said, crossing her arms.

He took a quick look over at her as she did so and focused his attention back on the treacherous highway. "Are you cold? I can turn up the heat."

Turn up the heat…

Little did he know he'd already done that with his charm, care, concern and his deep baritone voice that vibrated through her every time he spoke. Who was this guy? It took a special kind of person – man – to go all out of his way for a stranger. She for certain could never see Sariah's fiancé doing something like this. This was something a man like her father would do.

Growing up, her father set a fine example of the kind of man she wanted. Not only did he open doors for their mother – he opened the door for all women respectfully. He told his daughters: *a gentleman is not only a gentleman to the woman he loves. He's a gentleman always.* Dare was certainly giving off those gentleman vibes. She was sure some lucky woman had to have snatched him up. No way he was single.

With his fine self…

"Deja?"

"Oh, sorry. I was in a daze. Did you say something?"

"I asked if you wanted me to turn up the heat a little."

"No. I'm fine."

"Okay."

Up ahead, Dare saw the light change from yellow to red. He was already slowing down in advance, pumping the brakes carefully to successfully make the stop on the slick roads. "So, have you been there before?" he asked.

"Where?"

"The resort."

"Oh, no. I haven't. I heard good things about it, though."

"It's a nice place," he told her. "You're in for a treat."

"I doubt it," she mumbled under her breath.

"Why'd you say that?"

Gee…he heard her?

"Oh, um, only because I'm traveling solo. It's not exactly a *pleasure* trip. More like an unpaid work trip."

"Doesn't matter. You won't be working the entire time, and there are plenty of things to do. It's up to you whether you make it dreadful or fun."

"Is that right?"

"Sure it is," he said, his eyes crinkling at the corners. "Are you staying up on the mountains or in the valley?"

"That's a good question. My sister booked the condo so I don't know where I am. Given the situation, though, I hope I'm not up on the mountain."

"It's fine. They're excellent about keeping the roads clear up there. It shouldn't be a problem."

"Good."

Deja took in the scenery yet again. North Carolina didn't see much snow and some winters, it didn't snow at all. While the snow was a pain in the butt and presented many transportation challenges, she enjoyed the serenity of it. So, as they drove the rest of the way, she quietly took in the scenery.

Dare looked at her intermittently as she stared out of the window, seemingly in amazement. Right away, he surmised she didn't get out much. If she had, she would've dressed more appropriately for the weather. She had on a light jacket. No gloves, no hat and barely a pair of shoes. Those ballet flats didn't count. She didn't even have a hat or earmuffs. She would need all those things throughout the duration of her stay – that is unless she planned to spend as much time at the condo as possible. But where was the fun in that?

"Spotswood Trail must be the main road around here," she said.

"It is. It runs from Elkton to Harrisonburg and even further. The resort is right off of Spotswood."

Deja took note of the restaurants they'd passed – Thunderbird Café, Romano's Italian Bistro and Hank's Grille. She made a mental note of her dinner options.

WHEN THEY ARRIVED at the resort, she went to check in and was relieved when she realized she'd be staying in the valley. That meant she didn't have to worry about Dare towing her car up the mountain, or trying to navigate the high altitude herself when her car was finally repaired. She got her key and then Dare drove a few blocks down the street. When he found her building, he unhooked her car and released it. He had her sit in the driver's seat and with the car in neutral, he pushed it into a parking space so it wasn't in the other guest's way.

"Thank you so much," she told him. "You don't know how much I appreciate this."

"You're welcome."

"I don't have any cash, but I'd be happy to Cash App you some money."

"No, that's okay."

"Are you sure because I took a lot of your time and—?"

"I'm positive, Deja."

She dug in the front right pocket of her jeans and pulled out a twenty-dollar bill and said, "Oh, lookey…here you go."

He looked briefly at her hand and said, "Keep it. You need to buy some gloves." He looked down at her feet and said, "And some socks wouldn't hurt, either."

"I packed some socks. I had no idea I would need them. It was sixty-five degrees when I left Chapel Hill. I didn't know I was traveling to the frozen tundra."

"You didn't check the forecast ahead of time?"

"No. I was too angry to check the forecast. I just threw some stuff in the suitcase and hit the gas."

"I see. I'll get out of your hair now and let you get settled. Keep the money. If you insist on thanking me for towing your car, buy me a drink if you run into me again while you're here. Deal?"

Her lips curved upward as she extended her hand to him. He reached toward her with his gloved hand and shook hers.

"Deal," she said.

When their hands parted, he said, "Go buy some gloves, Deja from Chapel Hill."

"I will. Hey, do you know if there are any stores around here?"

"Not in this immediate area. There's a Walmart in Harrisonburg. That's the big city around here."

"That's why you live there, hunh?"

Dare relaxed into a smile.

Deja said, "Okay. Well, when my car is fixed, I'll head that way."

"Good."

"Thanks again, Dare."

"You're welcome, Deja. I'll see you."

Dare got in his truck and drove off.

Deja inhaled deeply, then fluttered her lips, making a *bbrrrrrrr* sound that sounded like a dirt bike. She looked at her car and said, "Okay, you hunk of junk...it's me and you now. You *better* behave when roadside service gets here."

Pulling her suitcase across the deep brown wooden ramp that led to a private entrance, Deja slid the keycard in the door slot to unlock it then stepped inside.

"Wow!' she exclaimed.

Her eyes landed on the large flat-screen TV mounted above the stone-encased fireplace in the spacious, beautifully decorated living room. A beige sofa set with a matching ottoman complemented the carpet with its accents of teal that blended with the pillows, wall art and lamps.

"This is…wow! I have a fireplace!"

She happy-danced her way down the hallway to discover a bathroom with a shower and a jacuzzi large enough to hold four people. The bedroom next to it housed two twin beds with the same teal color scheme as the living room: decorative teal pillows, and a teal curtain that was wide enough to cover both windows. She proceeded to the master bedroom.

"Eek!" she screeched with excitement and leaped on the bed. The mattress was so soft and fluffy, it took her entire body right in. The bed sat near a wall of windows. And…wait! There was a glass door. She hopped off the bed and opened the door to reveal a private balcony with a four-chair table, albeit covered in snow, but still. The balcony offered exquisite views of the golf course, well-maintained grounds and the postcard picture-perfect image of the mountains in the distance. She was still mad at her sister, but it looked like she'd enjoy being here for the week if she allowed herself to, just as Dare had said.

Dare…

A reminiscent smile came to her face since he'd crossed her mind already, remembering their frigid handshake. She'd promised to buy him a drink if they ran into each other again. What were the odds lightning would strike twice?

CHAPTER 2

DARE CALLED UP Dillon, his business partner and friend, to notify him he was running late. He'd been friends with Dillon since high school. Dillon was his *country* brother from another mother, he'd say, and he was definitely a country boy. He loved rocking his cowboy hats and boots. Dare was proud they'd remained close friends throughout the years, and now business partners. With all the fakeness on social media, you don't hear about people forming those lifelong friendships anymore.

"It's not like you to be late," Dillon said. "That GMC can plow through this snow like nobody's business."

"Yeah, well traffic was stop-and-go on 81."

"I heard. Did you get the tile samples?"

"I did. On my way back, I saw this woman stranded on the side of the road, so I helped her out."

"Ah, that's why you're late. There's a *woman*

involved."

"I couldn't leave a woman beside the road."

"Of course, you couldn't. You're Mr. Chivalrous."

"Dill, are you telling me you'd leave a woman stranded?"

"Nah, I wouldn't. I'm teasing ya, man. You did the right thing. How far out are you?"

"I'll be there in about fifteen. I dropped the woman off at Mass Resort, so that's where I'm coming from."

"I know. Ay, while you're out, why don't you grab some Popeye's. I could go for one of them chicken sandwiches."

"Alright."

Dare set the phone on the passenger seat, remembering Deja sitting there with her arms crossed. He knew she wasn't cold when she'd crossed them. It was probably just nerves, especially with being in a truck with a stranger. She didn't know she was safe with him, but that's who he was – the *safe* guy – not the bad boyish kind who women migrated to. Had he been one of those, he probably still would've been married. At any rate, he wondered, if by chance they'd meet again so she could buy him a drink. Something about her intrigued him. It would be nice to know what that *something* was.

* * *

"LOOKS LIKE THE weatherman was wrong," Dare said as Dillon opened the passenger door and got into the truck. "I didn't think we were supposed to get this much snow."

Dare unwrapped a chicken sandwich, then took a humongous bite.

"We weren't," Dillon replied, removing his hat, threading his fingers through his blonde hair. "We won't be able to do any outside work."

"Nah, not with it coming down like this."

The men continued eating. Dare turned up the volume on the radio when he heard a weather update. The weatherman was forecasting an additional four-to-five inches of snow to add to the four inches that had already fallen so far today and the three that fell the night before. And it was still coming down. He said, "I think we should call it a day."

"What do you mean by that?" Dillon asked after nearly chugging a Dr. Pepper in one swig.

"We can't work in these conditions."

"Well, I'll be—I don't believe what I'm hearing. You? The great Dare Stokes— homebuilder extraordinaire—is talking about calling it quits?"

"Ay, Mother Nature is forcing my hand at this point. When she talks, I listen."

"I find it mighty funny that you didn't listen a few days ago when the snow first started. Now, all of a sudden, you want to call it. You must have your mind on heading back over to the resort to check on your damsel in distress."

Dare lifted one side of his mouth to a half smile. It had crossed his mind a time or two. On the drive to Harrisonburg, he couldn't help but wonder if roadside service would show up. And even if they did, would they be able to help Deja with her car, or would she be stranded? He was no mechanic, but he knew a thing or two about vehicles.

He could slap himself for not leaving her his contact information or asking her for a phone number. At least he knew where to find her, but how would that look? A man who helped a stranded motorist ends up back at her doorstep while she's on vacation – yeah, not a good look at all. But how else was he going to see her again?

"The girl made *that* much of an impact on you?" Dillon asked.

"Let me clear something up. I'm not canceling work to go back to the resort to be with her. I don't know her. I just met her, Dillon. She's…um…interesting."

"I recall you saying the same thing about Heather."

Dare didn't say a word in response. Dillon should've known better than to bring up anything about that woman. Dare sat there thinking about Heather briefly – the woman who was his wife once upon a time when he believed in true love and happily ever afters. After ten years of marriage, Heather had left him. Said he wasn't *exciting* enough. He later found out she'd been cheating on him a year before deciding the other guy was everything she wanted in a man.

Dare balled up the wrapper from the sandwich and stuffed it into the takeout bag.

Dillon said, "It wouldn't hurt though."

"What wouldn't hurt?"

"For you to get back out there...find you a woman to put up in that mansion you built over in Winnbrook."

"That woman was supposed to be Heather. See how that turned out..."

"Well, she lost out. Everybody around here knows that."

"Nah. Everybody around here knows she made a fool out of me. I'm a laughingstock—"

"Dare, you're not. That's what you believe people think. But you know what—who cares what they think. We're out here making money and thriving."

"Yeah, that's true," Dare said because it was true. He was thriving and his business had taken off right around the same time his wife had taken off. But what was done was done. What sense was there in thinking about all of that now?

"Dare, if we ain't working, man, I'ma head on back to the house before it gets too bad out here. Miranda will be worried."

"Alright, Dill."

Dillon got out of Dare's truck, pulled out his wallet and placed a ten-dollar bill on the passenger seat. "This should cover lunch."

"Don't worry about it."

"Nope…I'm paying my way. Ay, what are you going to do? Are you gonna call it a day?"

"Yeah. I'ma stick around for a few to see if the snow will let up a little so I can unload these tiles."

"I can help you with that, Dare."

"No. Go home. You have a family waiting for you. I can handle it."

I have nothing to go home to, Dare thought. He had all the time in the world.

"You sure?"

"Yeah, man. Go. I got this."

"I'll come back out here first thing tomorrow morning to see how the tile looks with the granite countertop."

"Dillon, tomorrow's Sunday."

"Oh. Right."

"Enjoy your weekend. I'll see you back here on Monday."

"Alright, Dare. Take it easy."

"Yep."

Dare watched Dillon pull off and after he left, he finished his food, then put his gloves back on and unloaded the tiles. His company, Dare Homes LLC, was slated to build thirty new, single-family homes on the new property he'd acquired two years ago for two-million dollars. The land was excavated and cleared off earlier in the year and they'd already built five houses. Dare didn't want to throw up a bunch of houses that all looked the same and 'boxy' like most homebuilders were doing in the area. He wanted each home to have its own unique style, hence the reason he'd been riding around in a snowstorm searching for backsplash tiles. Having been in construction for nearly twenty years, he knew buyers loved an extra bit of *something* builders added to houses. It turned into a sale every time. With his attention to detail, he always knew what finishing touch to add to a house to secure an offer.

Too bad he couldn't put those same skills to use when it came to his personal life. It had been six years since his divorce and it still baffled him how he missed certain clues as to Heather's dealings. Everything was happening right under his nose. When he found out, it nearly knocked the wind out of him.

He sighed. That was over. It's *been* over.

But why was he not *over* it?

To get his mind off of it, he called his father.

Kevin Stokes answered, "Hey, there, son."

"Hey, Pops. I was calling to see how y'all were doing over there."

"Oh, me and your mom are fine—"

"Hey, Dare," his mother said in the background.

"Tell her I said hi."

"Wait, let me put you on speakerphone." After a quick moment, he said, "Okay, we're on."

His mother said, "Hey, Dare."

"Hey, Ma. I was calling to see if you and Dad needed anything while I was out."

"No, we don't need anything. I went to the store when the weatherman first told us all this snow was coming—let me tell you—most of the milk was already gone and I managed to get an off-brand loaf of bread by the skin of my teeth. What are you doing out in all of this mess? Don't tell me you're just now going to the store because I'm sure the shelves are all empty by this point."

"I was only going to stop if you or Dad needed something. I had Mrs. Jolene shop for me.

"She still helping you out around the house?"

"Yes. She's still there."

"Son, when I said you needed a woman around there, that's not what I had in mind."

"Carmen, if you don't leave that man alone about a woman," his father said. "Let him do what he needs to do."

"Mother, I'm fine if that's what you're concerned about."

"Okay. I'm just saying…you're over there by yourself in that big ol' house. Why don't you come stay with us—at least until the storm is over."

"No. I'm fine. As always, I appreciate your concern, but you have nothing to be worried about. Now, are you sure y'all don't need anything?"

His father said, "We're good, Dare. We got all the supplies we need until this thing blows over. We don't need to run out for anything. I tell you what, though—if I think of something, I'll give you a call."

"Sounds good," Dare told his father.

"And thanks for calling," his mother said. "If you change your mind, you know where to find us."

"Okay, Mother." His parents lived about eleven miles away in the small unincorporated community of Rawley Springs. When he was married, he and Heather would visit frequently, but he rarely visited them since the divorce. The memories were too painful, but not as painful as the expression on his mother's face every time she laid eyes on him. You'd think somebody died. She felt sorry for him – like he was nothing but *just a man* without a woman around.

Just a man…

A man with nothing to show for himself. Honestly, that's how *he* felt most days. He didn't need those constant reminders from his mother about the wife *vacancy* in his life. He had enough of his own problems.

CHAPTER 3

DEJA WOKE UP Sunday morning to back-to-back phone calls from her mother. Justine Barnett had a rule – if she called two times in a row, you had to answer the second call or call back within five minutes. Deja waited until minute *four* before she dialed her back.

Justine answered, "Sariah told me you made it okay. Thank goodness *she* called because trying to get you to call…shucks…I'll have better luck finding gold at the end of a rainbow."

"Ma, I was going to call you."

"Sure you were."

"I was. Sariah only knows I made it okay because I sent her a text message. I'm honestly surprised she had time to call you with her super busy schedule and all. Did she also tell you it's snowing polar bears over here? Did she tell you I almost got creamed by an eighteen-wheeler?"

"What!"

Deja continued while she was on a roll saying,

35

"Did she tell you my car blew the freak up and some random guy came to rescue me because I was on the shoulder of an interstate?"

"Aww…you were rescued by a stranger? How sweet is that?"

"Sweet? I didn't know him! Your daughter could be sweet and *dead* right now. This ain't one of your lil' happy-go-lucky movies, Ma. This is real life."

"Child, hush all that fuss. You're okay, aren't you?"

"I am now, but you don't even sound concerned. I'm here, and I'm stranded."

"Well, honey, be honest. You knew that pile of rusted metal you drive was going to die, eventually. Personally, I would have never taken a chance with that thing on a trip. Shoot, you put your life in danger every day driving locally. I thought for sure you'd get a rental for your trip, but anyway, I'm glad you made it. Won't He do it?"

Deja shook her head. Her mother was as bad as Sariah. That's why they got along so well. They both had this air about them. Things always seemed to fall in their laps and life flowed so easily. Honestly, she hadn't expected her mother to ask follow-up questions like, how did you get the car off the freeway in a snowstorm?

Justine proceeded to say, "So, the cake tasting is tomorrow. You'll need to be at the bakery at 9:00 a.m."

"I know, Ma."

"You can't be late, Deja."

"Or what? Am I going to get fired? It's a freakin' cake tasting. And, side note—why would anyone schedule a cake tasting first thing in the morning. On a Monday. It makes absolutely no sense."

"Honey, this ain't your wedding—"

"No kidding! Yet I'm doing all the work."

"Deja, just go with the flow. You know, as well as I do, that your sister's head will do a complete three-sixty if you're not there to taste those cakes."

"I don't care what Sariah's head does. I'm more concerned about my own freezing cold head right now. I'm just now starting to get the feeling back in my ears. And Ma—I just told you my car broke down and you didn't even ask me if I got it fixed so I can be in attendance at this gluttonous cake tasting event. All you're concerned about is that I'm there."

"Chile, who needs a car these days? You can take one of those rideshare doohickeys. You won't catch *me* in one, but y'all are from a different generation. Anyway, I'm glad you're safe, baby girl. Don't forget the cake tasting."

"Do you know where it's supposed to be? Sariah still hasn't texted me."

"Call her, Deja. Chow."

And then the line went silent.

Great.

Deja didn't have time to tell her roadside service was outside repairing the faulty water pump on her car. She was thankful they came out in the inclement weather. They'd probably hit her with an interesting 'service fee' to make up for it.

Deja dialed Sariah's number. It rang four times before the voicemail picked up. She immediately dialed again and the same thing happened. It rang four times, followed by voice mail.

She sent a text instead.

Sariah, hi, this is your SISTER who you left STRANDED. I would like to know where YOUR cake tasting is tomorrow, so I can taste cakes YOU will be eating at YOUR wedding! Call me back.

To Deja's surprise, she got a quick reply from Sariah:

Oh, boo-who...you're my maid of honor. You're supposed to be handling things like this for me.

Deja couldn't stand her sister's dismissive tone. She responded quickly, pounding the letters on the screen like a maniac.

Deja: Just tell me where the cake tasting is supposed to be.
Sariah: Ugh...hold on a sec. I'm looking it up...

Although she wasn't there, she could see Sariah rolling her eyes, huffing and carrying on like *she* was the one who had a right to be frazzled. After a few passing moments, her reply came:

Sariah: It's at Harrisonburg Bakery and Café. The address is 312 S. Main Street. If you need directions, Google it.
Deja: Why do you have an attitude? It's not like I should be doing this, anyway. I mean, what are you going to have me do next? Try on your wedding dress?
Sariah: Um, yeah! The appointment is on Wednesday at 9 a.m. Didn't I tell you that already??

"You have got to be kidding me," Deja said, sitting on the living room sofa staring at the unlit fireplace. She tried to call Sariah instead of doing all of this back-and-forth texting but her sister wouldn't answer the phone.

Deja: Call me RIGHT NOW or I'm not tasting no cakes or anything else!

Her phone rang immediately. When she answered, Sariah said, "You know Saturdays are my busiest days. I have like twenty open houses today."

"It's Sunday."

"Your point? In real estate, Sundays are like regular workdays."

Deja couldn't tell if Sariah was lying or telling the truth. Sariah always came up with excuses so she didn't have to do her own work.

Deja said, "First off, there isn't enough daylight in the world to do twenty open houses in one day. You can sell that story to somebody who's willing to buy it. And what do you mean I'm trying on your dress?"

"We wear the same size, Dej."

"But it's *your* wedding. You're the one marrying...*ugh*...Kris! Of all the men in North Carolina, you end up with Kris."

"Hush. Kris is a saint—"

"Kris is a weasel."

"A weasel with good taste. This ring he gave me is exquisite."

Deja rolled her eyes. "There's more to marriage than a stupid ring."

"How would you know?"

"Because I'm basically a stand-in for everything you're *supposed* to be doing for your wedding. That's how I know."

"Well, count your blessings instead of complaining. You need the practice for the *rare* chance you meet a man who can deal with all of your quirks."

"My quirks?"

"Yes. You know how you are." She chuckled softly. "Listen, I have clients asking questions. I have to get off this phone. Make sure you're at the bakery tomorrow. I hear they make some delicious cakes. Love ya. Bye."

Deja dropped her phone on the sofa and covered her face with her hands. "Why me?"

She blew a breath and said, "Okay, Deja. You're here now. You may as well pull yourself together. This is a nice place. Try to enjoy it a little in spite of everything."

So, that's what she did...

THE TECHNICIAN FINISHED the repair on her car by two, but with the weather still a mess, she wasn't about to go out for lunch. Instead, she ordered a pizza, flipped through the channels to find a movie and after settling on one, she turned on the gas fireplace. When the pizza finally arrived, she kicked up her feet, set the box on the coffee table and stuffed her face with carbs. She was officially in hibernation mode – that is until she had to leave her den to go taste some cakes in the morning.

CHAPTER 4

WITH A WORKING vehicle and a good night's rest, Deja headed to the bakery. The snow had stopped last night and fortunately for her, the hardworking transportation people were out early spraying the roads with brine to prevent them from icing. The sun shone brightly, but the temperature made it feel like the sun had no impact. It was a frigid thirty-nine degrees. The heat in her car was apparently on the struggle bus because it was blowing lukewarm air. Maybe it needed some time to recycle after the water pump repair. She had no clue.

Those gloves Dare told her to get would've come in handy this morning when she spent ten minutes trying to scrape frozen snow from her windshield with a dustpan and a wooden spoon while simultaneously keeping her eyes on two shady-looking deer grazing on the mountain across the parking lot. It's a sad day when one had to chisel snow with a wooden spoon, but what else was she going to do? She didn't keep an ice scraper in her car – didn't need to back home – but she would add that to her list of items to purchase after leaving the bakery.

Pulling up in the parking lot, she looked around the area, making sure she was at the right place. She checked the text Sariah had sent and looked at the sign on the building: Harrisonburg Bakery and Café.

"This is the place," she uttered softly.

The bakery seemed innocent enough. The picture of a cake and cup of coffee on the signage gave her a good feeling about this little café. She could smell bread and sugar wafting in the air, enticing her to come inside along with the delightful aroma of coffee. She could kill for a cup of coffee right now.

With her purse up on her shoulder, she carefully traversed the treacherous parking lot and made her way to the building. When she opened the heavy, wooden door, a bell sounded. The woman behind the counter, a sista, said, "Welcome. You must be the blushing bride."

Deja touched her cold cheeks and said, "Oh, no. I'm not blushing—I'm freezing. That's probably frostbite you see on my face."

The lady chuckled.

"And actually, I'm not the bride. My sister, Sariah Barnett, is the bride. I'm merely her scullion who goes to-and-fro taking care of stuff she doesn't want to do."

"Oooo-kay," the woman said, wide-eyed.

"Sorry, I shouldn't be telling you all this. Let me reset." Deja gathered in a long breath and released it slowly. "I'm Deja. It's nice to meet you…"

"Bonnie."

"It's a pleasure, Bonnie," Deja said, reaching to shake Bonnie's hand.

When their hands touched, Bonnie quickly snatched her hand back and said, "Girl, you're as cold as an icicle. How about I get you a fresh cup of coffee?"

"That sounds amazing. Thank you. I could use some coffee after the morning I had. I literally had to clean my windshield with a frying pan."

Laughing, Bonnie hurried to the back because this was what she considered an emergency. This girl was borderline losing it. She hoped the hot coffee would thaw out her brain so she'd level out a bit.

Returning with the cup on a tray along with some cream and sugar, she said, "Drink up….get that blood flowing again. The rest of your party should be here shortly."

"Thank you," Deja said, then took a sip. "Mmm…oh! I sooo needed this."

"You're welcome, Ms. Barnett."

"Please, just call me Deja. Ms. Barnett makes me sound like an old maid. Well, I am a maid, but I'm not old."

Bonnie giggled. "You're not a maid, darling."

Deja's eyes brightened. "Oh, I am *very* much a maid. Do you know my sister has me trying on a dress for her on Wednesday? Ridiculous, right?"

"Some women are not attached to their wedding like other women."

"Yeah, and I call those women delusional. If I was getting married, I'm tasting my own cake and trying on my own dress. *I'm* going to have a say in the decorations, the DJ—all that!"

"You sound like you'd be one of them bridezillas," Bonnie said, then chuckled.

"You know what, Bonnie. You're right. I'll admit it. I'm definitely bridezilla material." Deja gulped some coffee, then said, "Oh goodness. Please tell me you have more."

"Of course." Bonnie went back to the kitchen area to get her a fresh cup, brought it back out to Deja and said, "Here you go, hun."

"Thank you, Bonnie! Thank you!"

Bonnie shook her head, amused. "You don't get out much, do you?"

"How can you tell?"

"Well, for one, I know my coffee is delicious, but I don't recall it ever having anyone this excited."

"It's just been a hectic weekend, Ms. Bonnie. My car broke down on the way here and I didn't expect all of this snow. You could poke my big toes with a knife and I wouldn't feel a thing."

Bonnie looked down at Deja's shoes and said, "Honey, it ain't summer. You need to get yourself a pair of boots and some thick socks."

"Trust me—the items are already on my growing survival kit list. These Virginia mountains did not come to play, did they?"

"They never do."

"It's so beautiful here, though." Deja took another long sip of coffee and after it warmed her, she crossed her legs and asked, "Earlier, did you say somebody else was joining us?"

"Yes. Your soon-to-be brother-in-law and his plus-one."

The color drained from Deja's face. "You're kidding me."

"I'm afraid not. He called and confirmed it yesterday."

"Are you positive?"

"Yes. His name is Kris Stokes, isn't it?"

Deja could only shake her head in utter disgust. "I'm going to wring Sariah's neck."

"I take it she didn't tell you about this."

"No. I'm always the last to know everything and I talked to her yesterday. She knows I don't get along with her fiancé, with his cheap-looking face. This must be her way to force us to be friends, but I'ma tell you right now—it ain't gon' work!"

The doorbell chimed.

"Welcome to Harrisonburg Bakery and Café," Bonnie said.

"Hi, there, gorgeous," Kris said to Bonnie. "You must be the lovely lady who bakes the best cakes in the valley."

"That would be me," Bonnie replied, clearly blushing. What did these women find so charming about Kris?

Deja couldn't keep her eyes from rolling, so she tried closing them instead. Kris was good at flattery, flirting and foolishness. Deja couldn't stand how pretentious he came across, but Sariah didn't seem to mind it. She loved it. After three months of dating, Sariah said she was hooked on his *charm*, but from her vantage point, there was nothing charming about Kris Stokes. It took more than a fancy house and twin 2021 Range Rovers to charm her. Sariah, on the other hand, liked the way he lived and thus, he was a good match for her. She was a real estate agent – the best in the county, and he was the medical director at Durham Healthcare. With their combined incomes, they were supposedly *unstoppable*, Sariah had once said.

"Deja…how you doin' sis?"

Ignoring Kris, Deja asked Bonnie, "Are the cakes ready, because my nerves aren't set up for all of this?"

"Oh, don't go trying to run because I'm here, Déjà Vu," Kris teased.

Insulted, she snapped, "That's not my name!"

Kris loved referring to her as such because he knew it got under her skin. His soon-to-be sister-in-law wasn't what you would call *fond* of him. Poking fun at her was his way of wearing her down, so to speak, but it wasn't working. It never had before, but that didn't stop him from being more annoying.

He said, "Your name *is* Deja—"

"Exactly!" she said, cutting in. "That's my name. *De-ja*. Get it through that shiny, bald head of yours."

"Your sister loves this bald head, girl," he told her, taking off his hat, coat and scarf.

"That's only because her taste in men has always sucked."

"Until she met me. Ya boy got all this drip— how could she resist with her pretty little self. Mmm, mmm, mmm." He bit his bottom lip like he was fantasizing about Sariah.

Deja placed her index fingers on her temple and massaged them, but the motion did nothing to absorb her growing irritation.

Kris said, "Look, Deja...I'm sure we can put our differences aside for Sariah's sake, and if not for her, for the wedding."

"Personally, I'm still hoping, praying and wishing Sariah comes to her senses soon."

"Keep wishing. Sariah knows she'll never find another man like me."

"If she looked hard enough, I'm sure she could come up with something. Anything!"

"Will your brother be joining us?" Bonnie interrupted them to ask Kris.

"Yes, he's out in the parking lot." Kris slid his hands into his pockets, looked out the window and said, "Ah, here he comes now."

The door chimed. Deja didn't bother looking up. She sat there, irritated that she had to go through this. Sariah ought to have been ashamed of herself for this nonsense.

Kris said, "Bonnie, this is my big bro, Dare. Dare, this is Bonnie, our wonderful cake lady."

Deja's head immediately shot up when she heard Dare's name. Her mouth fell open. Dare – her interstate rescuer – was standing there next to Kris. Unbelievable!

"You," she said, surprise brightening her eyes.

Dare frowned a little, confused about why she was here, then he quickly connected the dots. Deja had told him she was here to handle some wedding business for her sister. Was her sister engaged to *his* brother? That couldn't be…

"Kris is your brother?" Deja asked Dare.

Dare's cheeks dimpled at the irony of it all. "Yes, he is."

"Wait," Kris butted in. "You two know each other?"

"Uh, um—" Deja stammered.

"Yes," Dare answered, a composed smile growing on his sexy, bearded face. "Somewhat."

"How's that possible, Dare, when you never leave Virginia?"

"I ran into Deja on Saturday. Her car overheated on the highway, and here you are," he said, soaking in her beauty.

"Yep. Here I am," she said, staring back at him

as intently as he was staring at her. She never thought she'd see this man again and here he was. What do you know? Lightning struck twice after all.

Kris looked at Dare then back at Deja noticing how the two couldn't seem to break eye contact and said, "Wow. Small world, huh, but then again, it's always been small for you, huh, Dare?" He chuckled and then told Bonnie, "He never goes anywhere."

Now Bonnie could see for herself why Deja didn't like Kris. She just met him and he was already getting on her nerves.

Dare was too busy staring at Deja to hear anything his annoying younger brother was saying. He noticed Deja looked different from when they'd first met. She wasn't frazzled. Her brown eyes stood out big and bright as she stared at him like he was too good to be true – almost as if he wasn't even there and she was imagining it all.

"Deja," Dare said.

She was still lost in a trance. Dare wasn't sure if she was aware he'd moved closer to the table where she was sitting.

Blinking out of a daze, she stood up and poked him in the chest with her index finger.

Dare glanced down at her hand, then back up at her face as humor touched his lips. "Yes, I'm really here if that's why you're poking me," he told her. "This is interesting, huh?"

"Very."

Deja's eyes took in the full scope of him. Why did he look taller than she remembered? And how on earth did she miss his magnificent amber-colored eyes and decadent, cappuccino-colored brown skin? He pulled off his toboggan, revealing a head full of thick, black, kinky hair that made him look exotic (as if his eyes weren't exotic enough already). Streaks of gray hair decorated his hair and beard, speaking to his maturity. When he took off his coat, Deja could see the print of his thick, beefy pecks through the candy-cane red Chaps sweater he had on – rocking it with dark blue jeans and a pair of honey-brown Timberlands. Was red his color or was he just that fly? Not only did he look good – he smelled good, too. Smelled like cedar and spices. Skip the cake – she was dying for a warm ginger snap cookie right about now, thanks to Dare.

"Deja," Bonnie said to get Deja out of another trance with Dare.

Deja had checked out of all conversations. Dare being here was like an ethereal moment – one in which she didn't know how to handle and so she stared and took it all in. Took him all in.

Have mercy…

"Deja, are you with us?" Bonnie asked.

"Oh, yes. I'm ready."

"Good. Y'all can follow me."

They followed Bonnie to a side room – the kind of room that looked like it could be used for small gatherings, but in this case, it was set up for Deja, Kris and Dare to stuff their faces with cake – plenty of cakes. This was cake paradise.

Bonnie said, "So, we have chocolate, vanilla, red velvet is a favorite for some, lemon, cheesecake and cupcake cakes."

"Cupcake cakes," Deja said. "That's a thing?"

"Yes," Bonnie said. "It has gained popularity over the last few years because you can get a variety of flavors in one cake. We arrange the cupcakes together to look like one, big cake. It's a hit."

Kris walked over to the cupcakes and picked one, taking a huge bite. "Mmm…this is…wow!"

"That's a vanilla cupcake," Bonnie told him

While Bonnie was busy offering Kris other flavors to try, Dare stepped closer to Deja and said, "This is awkward, huh?"

"Yeah. It's—I had no idea. What are the odds?"

"Yeah. What are the odds that the—how'd you put it—lil' *weasel of a jerk*, you described to me on Saturday was my very own brother?"

Deja dropped her head, embarrassed. "I'm so sorry. I had no idea—"

"Don't be sorry. That lil' weasel can be a jerk. Ever since he got that medical director position, it's like he took on a different persona—striving to be someone he's not."

"So, he's not really like this?"

"Well, he didn't use to be."

"Hey," Kris said. "Déjà Vu, come eat some of this cake, girl. Sariah sent me here to supervise, so get to tasting and leave my brother alone."

Deja inhaled sharply. She asked Dare, "Are you sure he's your real brother? Like, there's no room for doubt?"

Dare grinned. "Same mother and father."

"That's mind-blowing to me. I doubt Kris would stop to help a stranger beside the road."

"Probably not. He's not the help-a-stranger type. If it doesn't serve him, Kris isn't interested."

Bonnie looked up at Deja and Dare. "Come on, you two. The bride's countin' on ya."

"Are you sure, Bonnie?" Dare asked. "It looks like my brother has got it covered. You'd never know he was a medical director by the way he's tearing into those cakes."

Deja laughed. She liked Dare more and more already. "I guess sugar levels and whatnot doesn't matter when planning for one's wedding."

"No, it doesn't," Kris said. "Pleasing my wife is all that matters."

Deja stepped over to the cake table and listened to Bonnie talk about the chocolate cake like it was the best in the world. When Deja took a bite, she knew why. The cake was moist, and Bonnie had explained how she made everything from scratch, including the icing that melted on Deja's tongue.

"Oh, Bonnie, you've outdone yourself. Sariah is definitely going to want the chocolate," Deja told her.

"I think she'd go for the vanilla," Kris said.

"Please. I know my sister. Chocolate."

"And I know my wife. Vanilla."

"Correction, she's not your wife *yet*, Kris, and let's be honest. You've known Sariah for like seven minutes and a few seconds, so there's no way you'd know what cake she'd like."

"Okay, you two," Dare said. "How about we give them all a taste and narrow it down to the best three?"

"That's a good idea, Dare," Deja told him. She smiled, holding his gaze and a soft, but brief smile touched his lips.

"How in the world did you end up joining Kris for a cake tasting?" she inquired. "No, a better question is *why* did you join him?"

"He called me and said he was in town…wanted to hang out, so I decided to meet him here. Trust me, I didn't want to. I almost declined, but when I walked in and saw you, I was glad I didn't."

"I'm glad you didn't either."

"You know this means you owe me a drink, right?"

"Yep," she said, happiness dominating her features. He could have all the drinks she wanted as long as they get to spend time together.

Standing around the table, they tasted all the cakes Bonnie had made and narrowed it down to three. Deja chose chocolate. Dare was convinced the red velvet was the way to go and Kris liked the *cupcake* cakes – the variety option. It wouldn't be a bad idea, but as boujee as her sister was, Deja knew there was no way Sariah would go for cupcakes at her wedding reception no matter how *pretty* you made them look. Appearances were everything to her. She needed a super fancy cake – the kind of cake people would remember long after the wedding was over.

"Thank you for so much, Bonnie," Kris said. "This has been an excellent experience. I'll present my findings to Sariah, and we'll go from there."

"You're not presenting anything," Deja hissed. "Sariah specifically sent me here for this."

"I'm sure she'd like to hear from both of you," Dare said, continuing his impromptu role as mediator to defuse the tension between the two.

Deja looked at Dare. He was right, of course. She knew that. He was so much easier to listen to than Kris. She still couldn't believe they were brothers.

She said, "I have to get to the store. Bonnie, I'll be in touch after I talk to Sariah."

"Okay, Ms. Deja. I'll be waiting for your call."

"Yep, and since, my work here is done, I'm out."

"Alright, sis," Kris said to aggravate Deja even further. "See you on Wednesday."

"You won't see me no more this week." *Thank goodness!*

"I will. Sariah wants me to see the dress."

"What?!"

"Yeah, so like I said, I'll see you on Wednesday."

"Whatever," Deja huffed. "Thank you for your time, Bonnie."

"You're welcome. Don't forget to contact me as soon as the bride chooses which cake she wants."

"I will."

"*We* will," Kris said.

Deja grabbed her purse and exited the bakery as quickly as she could. As soon as she opened the door, the frosty air slapped her in the face, making her realize she'd left her jacket behind. She was about to go back and retrieve it when she saw Dare approaching her with it.

"Hey, you forgot this."

"Oh, thank you, Dare. You've come to my rescue yet again."

"I have."

"How's your car, by the way?"

Deja looked back at her car and responded, "It's running pretty good. Service came out and fixed it yesterday."

"Did they tell you what was wrong with it?"

"Yeah. I needed a new water pump."

"Ah, I see."

"I'm glad I got it fixed, though."

"I'm glad you got it fixed, too."

"Yeah...one less thing I have to worry about

because I certainly have plenty."

"I hear you."

She stared at him but quickly shied away not knowing what to say next if anything at all. He stared back with the same issue. He didn't know exactly what to say to her either, but he knew he didn't want this to be the last time they saw each other. She needed to know he was serious about those drinks. He said, "While you're at the store, you should probably get a hat, too."

She nodded. "It's on my list."

"Good."

"I know I've said this several times, but I can't believe Kris is your brother."

"Me either."

Deja laughed.

Dare smirked.

"He must get on your nerves, too," she said.

"When he moved from here and settled in Durham, let's just say I wasn't sad about it."

Deja laughed some more, prompting Dare's eyes to fall to her mouth. Why was he staring at her lips? Just then, he thought of doing something he'd never done before – he wanted to ask her out to dinner. He'd been thinking about her over the weekend and he knew she would be in Shenandoah Valley for at least a week, so why not? He knew why. He hadn't been out with a woman since Heather and had no desire to, but there was something urging him to ask Deja.

"Well, I'll see you around I guess."

"Yeah," he said. "I'll see you."

She walked away and he could kick himself. He still didn't have her number. He knew she'd be at the bridal studio with Kris on Wednesday, but how would it look if he showed up there? As it stood, Kris probably shouldn't have been there. There was something wrong about the groom taking a part in choosing his woman's wedding gown. Wasn't it a rule that the groom wasn't supposed to see his bride's dress prior to the wedding day?

Dare could certainly understand Deja's concern about her sister's upcoming nuptials. He had his own set of concerns about his brother. Kris had never come across as the marrying type. In the past, Kris had always juggled women. He wasn't convinced that Kris was ready to settle down, but if Sariah didn't have an issue with it, why should he?

The sound of a car starting snapped Dare out of his daydream. It was Deja. He scurried over to her vehicle and tapped his knuckles on the glass of the driver's side window. It was like déjà vu all over again. He grinned thinking about that.

Deja let the window down and said, "Did I forget something else?"

"Yes, I mean, no. You didn't forget anything. I…never mind. Have a good…day."

"Okay. Thanks. You, too."

She was about to put the window back up when Dare mustered up the courage to say what was on his mind. "Hey, you know I was serious about that drink."

She smiled. "Okay, so where should we go."

"If you're not busy tonight doing wedding stuff, maybe we could have dinner. I know a nice Mexican restaurant in Elkton that makes good margaritas."

A smile spread across Deja's face. "That would be nice and don't forget…it's my treat since you saved my life on Saturday."

"That's a stretch, Deja."

"No, it ain't. I was in full panic mode and because of you, I'm fine."

Dare cracked a smile. "I do what I can."

"And I appreciate all of it. Since you know where I'm staying, how about you come pick me up?"

"I'll be there around six."

"Perfect. I promise you I'll have some gloves by then."

"We'll see," Dare quipped.

Deja rolled up the window and backed out of her parking stall, then turned onto the street.

Dare smiled, feeling optimistic about spending time with her but at the same time telling himself it was just dinner. There wouldn't be much else to it. Besides, he didn't date after things had ended between him and Heather. It had been six years and the thought of dating another woman never crossed his mind. Was he holding on to Heather? His friends and family thought so. It was hard to move on when you thought the person you were with was the only one you were meant to be with. Unfortunately, Heather hadn't seen it that way.

"I saw you checking out Deja," Kris said.

"I get the feeling she's a good person to hang out with," Dare said casually.

"Sariah always jokes about her—says she's going to end up a forty-year-old virgin. She's so stiff."

"Wow. Her sister talks about her like that?"

"Yeah. It's just sister-talk, though. In my opinion, Deja is…ummm…I don't know what she is. I know she's not outgoing like her sister, and I know she doesn't like me."

"I think anybody can pick up on that, Kris."

Kris grinned. "But, what do I care? I'm not into her. I'm into her sister. Trust me when I say it's a night and day difference. Sariah is spicy, carefree, vibrant, and full of life. Deja's a wet matchbook."

"That's a terrible thing to say. You shouldn't talk about ladies like that, especially one who'll be your sister-in-law."

"Oh, kill the chivalry act, Dare. And there's no need for you to be on my case. Why don't you get out here and get yourself a woman instead of hoping Heather would come back? The woman said you were boring."

"I don't want Heather back. And since you brought it up, she didn't use to think I was boring before. How am I boring now? I build houses for a living. How's that boring?"

"It's boring to a woman. Do you think a woman cares about how many houses you build? I'll answer that for you. They don't."

"So, I should become a medical director to be interesting? Tell me what's so thrilling about your profession."

"It's not the profession. It's me. I go out. I have fun. I buy drinks. I'm the life of the party. What's the last fun thing you did?"

Dare shrugged. "I don't have much time for fun and games when I have deadlines to meet."

"Exactly. Look, I'm not saying you gotta be like me. You can't be like me. I got the sauce, brother," Kris said, popping his collar. "What I *am* saying is, you can loosen up a little, man, but you're certainly not going to do that with Deja, so don't waste your time."

Dare shook his head. Kris always thought he knew the answers to everything. Sometimes, he forgot Dare was the oldest – had him by seven years. He was wiser, smarter and better looking in his opinion. Kris got to where he was in life because he knew how to run his mouth and connect with people who knew how to run their mouths just as much. Dare wasn't the mouthy type. He was a man of action. A hard worker. A provider. Apparently, those things weren't good enough for women these days. According to Kris, they wanted more.

He told Kris, "I don't know how much advice

I should take from a man whose fiancée has him picking out a wedding dress for her. Later, bruh."

Dare walked to his pickup, started it up and returned to the housing development where Dillon and the rest of his team were waiting. He had a lot of work to catch up on before dinner with Deja.

CHAPTER 5

DEJA HAD CONSIDERED calling Sariah and telling her about Dare and their impending dinner date tonight, but she knew her sister would instantly complain about it. Sariah would see it as a distraction from Deja doing all the wedding prep. For that reason, she chose not to say a word. Everything wasn't about Sariah, but you couldn't tell her that.

Deja had dabbed on some blush when she saw the lights of Dare's truck through the large kitchen window. She put on her coat, boots, threaded her fingers into a brand spanking new pair of gloves, and headed outside. She still had to get used to vacationing alone, but Dare was a welcome distraction from the loneliness of it all. And today *had* been lonely, especially after she finished shopping. She ate lunch and took a two-hour nap. She woke up and fell asleep again while trying to watch TV.

When Dare saw her coming out of the condo,

he got out of the truck and opened the passenger door for her.

He said, "Be careful. The pavement gets pretty slick out here as night falls."

"Trust me when I say it doesn't need to be night for me to fall," she told him, taking his hand as she stepped up into the truck.

"You didn't fall today, did you?"

"I almost fell in the parking lot at Walmart. Do you know what saved me?"

"What's that?"

"The moves I learned from watching figure skating on TV, but trust me when I say it wasn't pretty. One leg went east, the other proceeded to go west, my body leaned south and I darted back north while struggling to maintain my balance. People were looking at me like I was crazy and they had every right to."

Dare chuckled and walked around the front of the truck to the driver's side. When he got in, Deja said, "You should've seen me. You would've been impressed or highly disturbed."

"I probably would've been impressed, especially if you were wearing those same shoes you had on Saturday."

"The flat ones. Yep, I was, but I got these boots now, so I should be good."

"Yes. You're good to go now."

As they drove away from the resort, the conversation tapered off. Deja wondered if that's how it would be at dinner, too. Awkward and quiet. Gladly, she was mistaken, because after a few sips of lime margarita, they both loosened up a little.

Deja looked around the place and saw a little girl at the table adjacent to theirs. The girl smiled, her cheeks full and beautiful as she rocked two afro puffs. She looked like she was about two years old. Deja smiled back and waved at her.

"She's so adorable."

Dare took a quick glance to see who Deja was waving at and noticed the girl who was sitting in a highchair with her parents and an older child. He thought they were a beautiful family – reminded him of the family he used to want. He flashed a half smile, then returned his attention to Deja. She was still exploring the restaurant, looking around at the walls and décor.

Deja spotted a purple sombrero hanging on the wall next to a window. She said, "I wonder if they got some extra sombreros around here."

"Why?" Dare asked, amused. "What will you do with a sombrero?"

"Have my own party."

After a quick sip of margarita, he asked, "Is that a regular thing you do? Solo parties?"

"Sure is. I dance while I'm cooking appetizers for my solo parties. Me and my apartment are inseparable."

Dare watched as Deja picked up the menu. He couldn't determine if some things she said, like being inseparable from her apartment, were meant to be taken as a joke. Did she spend so much time alone that she considered herself a solo partier? It wouldn't be so far out there. After all, he wasn't social by any means – only to the extent necessary. He, too, spent a lot of time alone.

At home.

Mainly doing nothing.

Unless staring at the walls contemplating his life's choices counted for *something.*

Deja asked, "What should I order here since you're a regular?"

"I'm not a regular. I haven't been here since—"

He stopped himself. He was going to say he hadn't been there since he'd gotten divorced but wasn't sure he wanted to talk about his personal life.

"You were saying," Deja said after taking a sip of margarita.

"Um…just that. I haven't been here in a long time." Dare picked up the menu and said, "They make good chips here, especially when they serve them hot. The chips can be their own meal if served with pico de gallo, cheese dip or guacamole."

"Then we'll have that for an appetizer. Is that okay with you?"

"Sure."

"What about dinner?"

"The fajita quesadilla is good and it's plenty."

"Then, I know what I'm getting," she told him, folding the menu closed, returning it to the table.

Once the food arrived, conversation temporarily ceased. The food was so delicious, there was no room for talking. Only eating. When they came up for air, Dare said, "Good, right?"

"Very!" Deja said. "And this thing is huge. I'm going to stuff myself trying to finish it."

"You don't want to do that. Save the rest for later while you're relaxing in your condo. How has it been staying there?"

"It's relaxing, warm and cozy. So far, it's the only part of my trip that doesn't suck. Well, that and spending time with you."

Their eyes locked and held. Deja smiled, but she didn't mean for her comment to sound so flirtatious. It was just a fact. Dare was the only person she knew there, well besides Kris and he didn't count.

Deja tore her attention away from his eyes and traced his nose and the shape of his lips instead. Handsome was unquestionably the word to describe him, but he was so much more. He was dreamy, super attractive, and yet he had this humbleness about him that made him much more appealing. It was a rarity to meet a man as good-looking as him who wasn't arrogant and full of himself. It made her wonder some things about him, like why he didn't have a ring on his finger, but this wasn't a date. This was dinner. She wasn't about to ask him twenty-one questions when they weren't trying to get to know each other on *that* level.

"It's funny how things work," Deja said. "I never thought I'd see you again and here we are having dinner."

"Yeah. That's how the universe works."

Deja narrowed her eyes. Did he really mean that, or was he just saying it? She decided to find out. "What does that mean?"

Dare had just taken a chunky bite of quesadilla and after chewing, he said, "It means when you do good things for people, it all comes back. People meet for a reason."

"And what reason did we meet?"

He stopped chewing and donned a subtle smile. "Maybe so I can help bridge the disconnect between you and my brother."

"Nah, that ain't it," she told him.

Dare grinned. "I think it is."

"So…what's there to do around here?"

He laughed. "Don't try to change the subject now."

"I'm not."

"That smile on your face says otherwise."

"I promise, I was just asking. To keep my sanity, I'm trying to fill my days with activities that don't involve anything wedding-related." *Or Kris-related.*

Dare's phone rang. On instinct, Deja snuck a look and saw a woman's name come up on the display. Jolene.

"I'm sorry. Excuse me for a moment." He picked up the phone. "Hey, Jo…yes, on the kitchen counter…okay, be safe out there. Bye."

Dare placed the phone back on the table and said, "Sorry about that."

"No worries," Deja said. It was the first time she considered that Dare wasn't some lone, handsome man without an attachment. He seemed to be pretty friendly with whoever Jolene was.

But that's none of my business.

They had no expectations of each other and she'd be a fool to think he was interested in her because of their wild circumstances – the snowy tow ride he gave her and the fact that she discovered he was Kris' brother. She would enjoy this dinner with him and go back to handling her sister's affairs.

"Activities," he said picking up where they'd left off, "The resort should've left an activity booklet in your room. They have plenty to do over there. You haven't seen the huge indoor waterpark yet?"

"Waterpark?"

"Yes. There's a waterpark. You have to drive there from your building. When you get there, you can change into your swimsuit, play around for a while and then when you're done, you change back and head to your car."

"But it's like Frosty-the-Snowman degrees

outside. If I did something like that, my nipples would probably freeze off and roll around like marbles right there in the parking lot before I'm able to make it back to my car. I'm doing pretty well for myself, but I doubt if I can afford nipple reattachment surgery."

The subdued smile on Dare's face became all-out laughter. When he was finally able, he asked, "What the heck are you talking about?"

She giggled at her own silliness. "I'm just saying…"

Dare asked, "You say whatever comes to your mind, don't you?"

"What? You act like that can't happen."

"It can't," he said, still tickled. "It won't."

"Well, I don't want to find out. Waterparks and winter don't mix. At some point, you have to face the fact that summer's over."

"If you only went…you might be surprised, Deja. You said you were looking for activities to do. Try it."

She shrugged. "I don't know. Maybe."

"What about the ski lift?" he inquired.

"I can't ski."

"Oh, now the parking lot figure-skater claims she can't ski."

Deja cackled.

"Okay—what about snow tubing?" he tossed out.

Deja finished the rest of her margarita and said, "I rode up the mountain today and saw so many people out there tubing. I immediately told myself I wasn't going to be one of those people."

"Why?"

"Because hiking up a super-long flight of steep stairs only to go sliding to my death down a snowy mountain on a glorified pool noodle isn't exactly my idea of fun."

Dare's wide smile turned into a chuckle. "You're something else."

"I'm dead serious."

"I know you are. That's what makes it funny. It's also why I'm taking you snow tubing tomorrow."

"No, you're not."

"I am."

She raised a defiant brow. "How do you figure?"

"Easy. Tomorrow, after I get off work, I'ma drive over to the resort, pick you up and we're heading up the mountain."

"Do you think I'm going to do whatever you ask because of your good looks and charm?"

"No. I'm not trying to charm you, Deja."

"Why are you looking at me like that then?"

"Like what?" he asked, tickled.

"*That*—that weird thing you're doing with your eyes. They change appearance based on the lighting."

"I'm not doing anything but looking at you. That's just my eyes."

And they were some beautiful ones, sparkling

like diamonds beneath the light in the restaurant. She wouldn't mind spending more time with Dare. If he wanted to go snow tubing, she was down with it.

She said, "I know this isn't a get-to-know-you kind of situation, but I'm curious—what kind of work do you do?"

"Guess."

"Um…I don't have the slightest idea."

"Take a guess," he said again and sipped his drink. "I'm curious to see what you come up with."

"Okay, um…let's see…um…I don't know. You could be anything."

"Okay, then throw something out there."

"Ummmmm…." She picked up a chip and took a bite of it like it was helping her think. She said, "You're a painter."

"Not a bad guess," he said. "I build houses. I know it's not *exciting*, but I enjoy it."

"What do you mean it's not exciting? *You* get to build houses that people will spend their lives living in, raising their kids, *making* their kids and being happy. It should be very fulfilling and exciting work. I can't build a Lego house from scratch, let alone a *real* one. That takes some real talent. I'm impressed."

"Thank you," he said. Too bad Heather hadn't seen his profession in that light. Or maybe it wasn't the profession at all. She just fell out of love with him and into the arms of another man.

"How long have you been in construction?"

Dare blinked out of his thoughts and responded, "A long time. I knew early on that I wanted to go into business for myself, so Dare Homes LLC was born."

"How inspiring is that? It's so cool that you went for it. I wish I was brave enough to start a business."

"What do you do, Deja?"

"I'm a virtual assistant. Now *that* is boring."

"How so?"

"I sit on my butt all day helping my clients *further their business interests*," she said, using air quotes. "That's why it's flat."

"What's flat?"

"My butt."

"Gee," he said, leaning back, laughing.

"It's true. I need to buy that squat machine I see on social media all the time. It's supposed to help with that."

"Wow. Okay."

"Sorry. Too much information, huh?"

"Nah, you're good. Your candidness is refreshing."

"Why thank you, kind sir."

"You're welcome, Deja."

Deja ate a few more chips. She'd already decided to save the rest of her fajita for later.

"How many clients do you usually take at one time?" he asked.

"Right now I have five, but I've had as many

as ten at once. It takes a lot of planning and scheduling. Most of them only want social media management."

"How do you have time to handle all this wedding stuff for your sister?"

"I have my laptop with me. I can work from anywhere. Sariah, on the other hand, is a real estate agent. She has to be in person with her clients, so I was the solution to her problem."

"I see."

The waitress came by. Deja requested a to-go container. Dare didn't have any food left. He surprised himself that he was able to finish the fajita, but after the cake tasting, where he barely sampled any of them, he skipped lunch and put in a full day's work. This meal was right on time and as for the drink – he was finishing the margarita. He was finishing up the little margarita he had left.

Deja used a straw to finish hers. She felt like the room was spinning after she was done sucking it all down.

"Oh my…you're going to have to help me walk out of here, Dare."

"Surely you're not tipsy off of one margarita."

"I am…a tad bit. This is a huge glass."

Dare took out his wallet.

Deja said, "Nope. Put that away. I'm paying."

"I'm not about to let you pay for all of this."

"All of what?" she asked. "We got two drinks, two dinners and one appetizer. I told you it was my treat. It's the least I can do for everything you've done for me."

"Well, I did what I did, and I wasn't expecting anything in return from you, but I appreciate the gesture."

Dare placed seventy dollars in the billfold, then stood up and put on his jacket. He reached for Deja's hand. She took it and, with his help, was able to stand without feeling like she'd fall right back down into her seat.

After he assisted her with her coat, they walked hand-in-hand to the door. He pushed the door open, allowing her to exit ahead of him and when she did, the cold, unforgiving mountain air slapped the buzz right out of her.

With chattering teeth, she said, "These frigid temps are making the fifty-five degrees back home sound like summer."

"Yeah, that's how it is up here, but you're only here for a week—well, less than a week now."

"I guess I shouldn't be complaining, especially since you're stuck here all the time."

"I wouldn't say *stuck*. This is my home. I'm used to this. It's all I know. Plus, we have a nice summer, spring and fall around here. It's only the winter months that are challenging."

"I see."

Dare helped her into his truck, and they headed back to the condo.

WHEN THEY TURNED on her street, Redstone Lane, a deer galloped across the road.

"Whoa!" Deja said as Dare hit the brakes. "Is there a deer infestation around here or something?"

He chuckled. "Why do you ask?"

"You almost mowed one down just now, and I saw two of them watching me this morning."

Dare laughed a little more and said, "I'm sure they weren't *watching* you, Deja. There are a lot of deer around here. This land was theirs before it was taken over by the resort."

"I guess."

Dare parked and helped Deja migrate safely from the truck to the door. She smiled, and said, "We made it."

"Yeah, we did."

"Thank you for dinner."

"You're welcome, Deja." Dare offered a quick smile, then said, "I'll let you get inside. It's cold out here."

"Okay. Goodnight."

"Goodnight, and remember, I'm taking you tubing tomorrow."

"Nooo, Dare? I thought you were joking."

"I wasn't. I'll be here at two."

"Two o'clock?"

"Yes."

"But aren't you working around that time?"

"I'm taking the afternoon off," he told her. That's something he usually never did. Since

Heather broke his heart, one thing he could rely on to keep himself sane was his steady work, but tomorrow, he'd interrupt that long work streak for a chance to spend time with Deja again.

"Okay. I'll be ready."

"Alright. Goodnight."

"Goodnight, Dare." She stood there watching him walk back to the truck. Before he reached it, she said, "Watch out for the deer."

He gave a lopsided grin. "I will."

CHAPTER 6

THE MORNING SUN rose beautifully over the Blue Ridge Mountains, brightening the day and the light blue sky, but didn't do a thing to melt the snow. Even if it prompted a little melting action, there was more snow in the forecast. According to the weather report she heard last night, they were in for a doozie come evening into night. She'd have to chisel her car free again in the morning to make it to Sariah's wedding gown appointment. At least she had an ice scraper this time.

Sariah had called last night as Deja was getting into bed, but she didn't bother answering. She was certain Kris had already told Sariah about the cake tasting and put his own flair on things. That's usually what he did.

After warming up with a cup of coffee, she called Sariah to discuss the cakes. She didn't want to, but what other choice did she have?

Sariah answered, "OMG…'bout time you

called me back. What is this I hear about you coming to the cake tasting with Kris' brother?"

Deja shook her head. That's why she didn't answer Sariah's call. She had a hunch that some nonsense was brewing behind the scenes. "See, I knew Kris was going to call and tell you some mess. I didn't *show up* with his brother. I was the first one to arrive."

"Then how do you know Dare?"

"Remember when I was broke down beside the road on the way here? When you didn't do a thing to help me? Left me stranded? Remember that?"

Deja took a sip of coffee, listening to Sariah's long sigh.

Deja continued, "Dare was the guy who helped me. I had no idea he was Kris' brother. How would I have known that? I don't even know Kris, so there was no way I'd know his brother."

"You *could* get to know Kris. You don't want to know him."

"Duh."

"He's going to be your brother-in-law, Deja."

"That's unfortunate."

"Deja!"

After a sip of coffee, Deja said, "You should've seen how Kris was tearing up those cupcakes like he came to the cake tasting for the sole purpose of satisfying his sweet tooth."

"Oh, trust and believe I'm enough for all his

teeth."

"Are you sure, because he dived into that cupcake cake head-first like sugar had just been invented?"

"Did you say cupcake *cake*?"

"Yes. It was one option. It's a cake made of individual cupcakes—different flavors. Kris didn't tell you about it?"

"No. He said he was going to wait until you talked to me first. You know that's so not my style."

"That's what I told Kris, but he said it was. I don't even know why you sent him to the bakery, Sariah."

"He had some free time. He's in town hanging with his parents, so I thought, ay, why not?"

"Most likely, you're trying to force me to get along with him, but it ain't happening. He gets on my nerves so bad."

"But I guess his brother swooped in and made everything alright, huh?"

"Sure did. He rescued me and my car."

"Yeah, well, I think there are a few things you need to know about your snow *bae*."

"He's not my—"

"Shh…listen, Deja. I'm telling you this 'cause I love ya. Now, you may want to stay away from Dare. Kris told me that Dare's wife left him for another man, girl. According to Kris, he's been a little *off* ever since, if you catch my drift. If you ask me, he might've been cuckoo all along. That's probably why his wife left him in the first place."

"You can't be serious," Deja said to Sariah's vitriolic attack on a man who's soon to be her brother-in-law.

"Oh, but I am. Just watch out."

"How about *you* watch out? You need to be alarmed by a man who so easily throws his brother under the bus. If what Kris done ran back and told you was true, do you think Dare would want his business out in the street like that? And what kind of man would talk about his brother like a dog?"

"He was telling me because he was concerned."

"No, he was telling you because it was *something* to gossip about. See, that's why I don't like him."

"Look, Deja—I gave you the information. It's up to you what you do with it. Don't let your naivety get you mixed up with somebody who ain't got it all together."

Deja frowned. Feeling like she had to defend Dare, she asked, "Have you ever *met* Dare?"

"No, but I trust what my fiancé has to say about him. It's his brother. Who would know him better than his own brother? If Kris says he's unstable, how can I argue with that?"

"You shouldn't judge people based on something you heard. Nothing about Dare comes across as unstable. He's certainly got more sense than Kris. That, I'm sure about."

"Whatever. You don't like Kris. Never have.

That doesn't mean you can dismiss what I'm saying. Kris says Dare has never entertained a woman after his wife bounced. You know, some people can't handle the end of a relationship. They get all psycho."

"We don't know the circumstances, Sariah. That's Dare's business."

"All I'm saying is, be careful. If you were focusing on what you're *supposed* to be doing, you wouldn't have time to be hanging out with him."

"Right, because doing *anything* besides what you want me to do is unacceptable. Pretty soon, I'll need your permission to breathe."

"Oh, stop with the drama, Deja."

Again, Deja found herself wanting to end the call, but she decided to sip coffee and not give a second thought to her sister's nonsense.

Sariah said, "Are you still on the line?"

Unfortunately. "Yeah. I'm here."

"Let's move away from talking about Dare because you won't be seeing him anymore, right?" Sariah paused and waited for Deja to answer and when she didn't, she answered for her. She said, "Right. So, what cake did you like?"

Begrudgingly, Deja replied, "The vanilla cake was the best—vanilla cake with buttercream frosting."

"Awesome. I'll call Bonnie tomorrow and let her know to go with the vanilla."

"I bet you will," Deja mumbled.

"What was that?" Sariah asked.

"Nothing, but you know what? I think you should be doing this stuff yourself, especially trying on the dress. Can't you take the day off? I mean, Kris is already here and—"

"No can do. I'm about to close on a million-dollar property. That's a hefty commission for me. There's no way I'm missing out on that deal."

"Just so I'm understanding…the *deal* is more important than your marriage."

"That's *not* what I said."

"Well, that's what I heard." Deja took a deep breath. To get off the phone with her sister, she said, "I got a beep. I have to go."

"I didn't hear a beep."

Click.

Deja ended the call. It never failed – talking to her sister proved exhausting every time. Sariah didn't appreciate a thing, and while Deja shouldn't have been surprised, it still came as a shock sometimes.

Deja had always lived in her sister's shadow. She was so used to it, she simply tolerated her second-place position. Their parents (their mother mostly) had Sariah up on a pedestal since she was old enough to walk. Deja was two years older than her and even though they could pass for twins, Sariah was dubbed the slightly better looking one. The one with the better job. The one who was most likely to get married first. She dressed so exquisitely and ladylike. You'd think she was a millionaire by the way she lived.

The main difference between the siblings was their attitudes. While Deja was down-to-earth, Sariah walked around like she dripped glitter with every step she took. She loved to flaunt her lifestyle, her accomplishments and especially the fact that she was engaged. It was always, 'hey, look at me', as if her worth was determined by how many outsiders thought she was successful.

Deja couldn't understand it. It didn't take all that for somebody to be happy and satisfied with their life. When it came down to it, *you* were the one who had to live that life. And that's what she was trying to do – live hers – without her sister constantly throwing her success in her face like she would never get married or have a house, or drive a nice car – one that wouldn't leave her stranded on the interstate.

CHAPTER 7

DEJA WAS NEVER one to listen to what other people had to say about *other people* because if she wanted to know something about someone, she preferred to learn all on her own. She could only imagine the things she'd hear about Sariah from a third party if Sariah wasn't her sister, so who was she to put any stock in what Sariah had to say about Dare?

She glanced over at him. Dare had picked her up a few minutes ago and, while they headed up the mountain to the ski area of the resort, she couldn't help but think about what Sariah had said about Dare.

Contrary to what her sister thought, she wasn't naïve. She knew how to read people and protect herself. She'd gotten nothing but good vibes from Dare from the start. Even now, sitting in the truck with him, she didn't feel any kind of threat. Being with him felt like she was with…

A friend.

She *was* with a friend.

After all, he didn't have to stop and help her when her car broke down, but he did. Kris wouldn't have. He was too hung up on himself to be concerned about the welfare of somebody else. That's who Sariah needed to be worried about. Then again, Sariah wasn't far from him. That's why they got along so well. Why they made a good couple and were getting married. They were birds of a feather, and they were certainly flocking together.

Dare glanced over at her and said, "You're unusually quiet this afternoon."

Deja sighed inwardly. "I have a lot on my mind, especially after talking to my sister this morning."

"What does she want you to do now? Marry Kris for her?"

Deja cackled, falling back laughing. "That's a good one, Dare."

He only grinned a little.

Deja said, "I talked to her earlier today. She was...you know...being her."

"How so?"

"Um..." Deja cleared her throat. "Talking a bunch of nonsense. Said I wasn't focused on what I came here for, and the only reason she said that is because Kris told her I was spending all my time hanging out with you."

"I knew he would say something. That's Kris. To your sister's point, though, you have been spending a lot of time with me. I think you like me."

Dare glanced at her quickly as he turned into the parking lot.

Deja's cheeks darkened a shade. "I wouldn't be with you right now had you not coaxed me into doing this snow tubing nonsense."

"But you came," he said, pulling into a parking space large enough to accommodate his truck. "Because you wanted to." He shifted the gear into park, then turned to the right to look at her, catching her smile and those bright eyes that bore into him.

"Okay, Dare. I see what's going on here."

He chuckled. "Then tell me because I don't know."

"You're taking my sister's side and Kris' side. I'm all alone in this world."

"No, I'm playing around with you," he said, placing his right hand on her left thigh. She looked at his hand, then looked at him, more specifically at his lips.

Why was she looking at his lips?

Stop looking at his lips, she told herself. She forced her eyes straight ahead.

"Are you ready?"

"Yeah. It's all *downhill* from here. Get it?"

"You'll be okay," he said, opening the door to get out.

"Yeah, as long as I have my protector with me," she mumbled while she watched him walk along the front of the truck, coming to assist her. He pulled the door open, took her hand, and once she was standing on the ground next to him, he closed the door.

They walked up to the booth to pay. Dare took out his wallet, covered the fees and after getting tubes, they made their way up the steep stairs, listening to other thrill-seekers scream and holler on their way down the slippery slope.

"My nerves are not set up for this."

"You'll be fine, Deja. I'll be right behind you."

"No. I have to be behind *you*. You're bigger and stronger than I am. I don't want you flying down the hill behind me. It'll be like a tractor-trailer colliding with a Volkswagen Beetle. I'm coming out on the losing end of that battle."

"It won't be a collision. If anything, I'd only bump you a lil' bit."

"Yeah, and who says I want to get bumped?"

Dare grinned, amused by Deja's reluctance.

Once they were at the top, the worker held the snow tube so Deja could properly position herself on it.

"Alright. Are you ready?" the worker asked.

"Nope."

"Okay, here goes," he said as if he hadn't heard her and gave her a push.

"Ahh," Deja yelled as she began her descent down the hill, but when she finally stopped yelling, she realized how fun this was. It was cold as all get out, but it was a fun ride down.

Once she came to a stop, Dare bumped into her as he predicted he would.

"That was awesome, wasn't it? Wow!" Dare exclaimed.

"Wait...don't tell me this is your first time doing this."

"It is," he replied with a sly grin on his face.

"What! All that talking and convincing you did for me to come out here and it turns out you're a virgin, too? I thought you were speaking from experience."

He chuckled as he stood up, picking up the tube in the process. He reached for her hand to help her up as well. "If I told you I'd never been, you wouldn't have agreed to come with me. Am I right?"

"Absolutely!"

"See, that's why I didn't tell you."

"That's so wrong."

"How's it wrong when you still had a good time?"

"Mmm...I guess you got a point."

"Let's go again," Dare told her. "You down?"

"Yeah. Let's do it. I'm sure I'll be a little more relaxed this time."

They were down the hill yet again and this time, Deja didn't scream bloody murder on the way down. She was getting pretty good at this snow tubing thing.

After a few more trips down, they sat on a bench and rested for a moment.

"I hope you're enjoying yourself as much as I am," Dare said.

"I am. I'm glad you suggested this. I made it without breaking any bones."

"That's always a plus, isn't it?" Dare asked.

Deja laughed. "Absolutely."

"What are you doing for dinner?"

"Oh, I'm not eating dinner this evening. I got some carrots I'll snack on, but that's about it."

"Carrots? You're kidding, right?"

"Nope."

"That's all you're having for dinner?"

"Yeah. I have to try on Sariah's wedding gown tomorrow. I can hear her rude comments now if the thing can't zip all the way up."

"That's all the more reason for *her* to be here trying on her own gown."

"Exactly. Can you tell her that for me, please, because I can't seem to get it through her head?" Deja rubbed her gloved hands together. "I can't believe how cold it is out here, even with all this gear on."

"I bet you're glad you bought those boots and gloves, though."

"Yes! And I got an ice scraper. You should've seen me trying to clean my windshield with a spoon...definitely not my best moment."

"I can only imagine."

Deja sniffled and said, "Question—if you've never done this before, what kind of activities do you usually get into around here?"

He shrugged. "This is a resort. There's plenty to do. Did you ever find the activity booklet in your condo?"

"I'm not talking about the resort. I'm talking about you."

"Oh. I don't get into much. All I do is work, mostly."

Thinking about what her sister had told her this morning about Dare, she wanted to ask him about relationships *without* asking him about relationships. She went with, "How's the dating scene around here?"

"I wouldn't know anything about that."

"No?" she asked. "You don't date?"

Because a man that fine had to date…

"No. I haven't been interested in dating. Hanging out with you is the closest I've come to dating in quite some time."

"Oh. Okay." That got her to thinking – if he wasn't dating, who was Jolene and why was she at his house? She said, "I'm no better. When I'm home, I'm in my bubble and I stay there, do my work and only leave my apartment to buy the necessities—sort of like I've been doing since I've been here."

"Except for snow tubing, huh?" he asked.

"And dinner last night," she said.

"Right." Dare stood up and rubbed his gloved hands together. "Well, I guess we can go now to get you back in the warmth of your condo. Have you used the fireplace yet?"

"I've used it every single day. It's very relaxing. I wish I had one in my apartment now. I'm thinking about buying one of those fake ones. What do you think about those?"

Dare shrugged. "I think the ones that are actual heaters are functional and adds value to the space. The ones that are simply for the illusion of a fireplace—I don't like those."

They returned to his truck. He cranked up the heat after they were comfortably inside.

"Ah, that feels good. It's funny how in the summer, we don't want anything to do with the heat, but in the winter, heat is our friend."

"That's the way it goes," he said, making his way down the winding mountain road. A short drive later, he pulled up to the condo and slid the truck into park, then shut off the engine.

"Oh, you don't have to get out, Dare. I'll just make a run for it."

"No, let me get the door for you."

He got out and, as usual, walked around the truck to open the door for her.

"Thank you, kind, sir," Deja told him.

"You're welcome."

He held out his arm so she could lock her arm around his as they walked to the door. When they stepped up on the ramp, Deja said, "Thank you for inviting me. I had fun, and I didn't die."

"That's always nice."

She snickered as they came to a stop in front of the door. She unlocked her arm from his and rubbed her hands together.

"Alright, get in there and warm up. Eat some carrots for me."

Deja smiled. "I will." She found herself standing on her tiptoes, attempting to kiss him on the cheek. Dare darted his head away to avoid contact with her lips.

"Oh…sorry," Deja said, embarrassed. "Um, let me get inside." She unlocked the door quickly, entering the condo and closing the door behind her faster than she had entered. Leaning up against it, she said softly, "Why did you try to kiss him, Deja? Ugh…so embarrassing."

Dare stood there motionless. He wanted to knock on the door and apologize for moving away from her like she had the cooties, but he finally walked away and went back to his truck, doubtful he'd talk to her again.

But did he really want to?

Did he think something could grow between him and this beautiful woman who was from out of town? Not likely. But he liked her. She was different. And funny – a pleasure to be around. He liked that. What he *didn't* like was the uncertainty of relationships. In relationships, you had to trust the other person. After what had happened to him, he didn't trust anyone and doubted if he ever could. He was better off like he was – single and not ready to mingle. His life was construction, and that's where he decided his focus should be – not on the intriguing woman

TINA MARTIN

from North Carolina.

CHAPTER 8

"HERE'S THE DRESS!" the bridal boutique stylist said, marching in the room holding the wedding gown in her arms as if she was carrying a small child to safety. It was a wedding gown for goodness sake. A glorified dress embellished with beads so the boutique could charge a boatload of money for it. This particular one cost $8,000. Why would anyone pay that much money for a dress they would only wear once? It was beyond Deja's comprehension, but not out of the ordinary for Sariah. It fit right in with her sister's expensive lifestyle.

The woman flipped her silky, ash-blonde hair and said, "I'm Winnie, by the way."

And Winnie was a loud talker.

"You said, Winnie?" Deja asked. "Like Winnie the Pooh?"

She cackled. "Yes, just like the bear, hun, but I don't like honey, although my hubby says I'm sweet like it, so there's that." She waggled her brows.

Deja looked at her sideways.

"I'll be right here to help you every...step...of...the...way," she said and did a little march to reinforce her words. "Don't you worry your pretty little face about a thing! First, I need you to confirm that this *bea-uuu-ty* is the gown we're trying on today."

Deja shrugged. "I guess so..."

"You guess? Oh, it looks like somebody's gettin' those wedding day jitters. A little coffee will knock them right out of your system. I know you're excited about your big day, hun!"

"I'm not," Deja said, just to see Winnie's reaction.

The smile fell from Winnie's face. Crestfallen, she asked, "You're not getting cold feet, are you?"

"I'm going to be honest with you—my feet have been cold since I've been here Winnie."

"Oh, my word. Well, can I ask what's the matter?"

Deja laughed and then explained, "I was just messing around with you, although my feet have been cold since I've been here. However, I'm not the bride. I'm her maid."

"Oh. You're the maid of honor?"

The disappointment on Winnie's face couldn't be mistaken for anything else.

"You say maid of honor—I say *maid*, and I mean that in every sense you can think of."

Winnie offered a confused chuckle. "So, the bride is on the way still, or—?"

"No, Winnie. The bride, who is also my lovely sister, Sariah Barnett, has more important things to take care of, so she sent me to try on the dress for her."

Winnie's face twisted. "You're pulling my leg, aren't you?"

"Unfortunately, I'm not. I'm supposed to model the dress for her while she's on video chat."

"Are you two the same size?"

"No, she *thinks* we're the same size, but I'm pushing a size twelve. She's a ten."

"Oh boy. This dress is an eight."

"A what!"

"No worries. Before we panic, let's go back in the changing room and give it a whirl!"

"Alright, but when I bust out of this thing—"

Winnie giggled. "You'll be fine. I know you will."

Her optimism wasn't rubbing off on Deja. Still, she stepped into a dressing room, stripped down to her undergarments and immediately began shivering. "My goodness, it's cold in here. Do y'all have the heat turned on?"

"We do, but since you're here early, the building hasn't had time to get all warm and toasty. Sorry about that, hun."

Deja looked at the dress and shook her head. A size eight…

She was sure she could get one leg inside, but two? That was asking too much.

"You alright in there, hun?" Winnie inquired.

"Ye-yeah, I'm good."

But she wasn't good. Sariah always had her getting into some mess. It was a challenge to come here and try on the dress for her sister to start with, but trying to squeeze her butt into a size eight was asking too much for her curves and her sanity.

She wiggled the dress up her legs. It tightened at the base of her thighs and stayed there like it was paying rent. Deja tried the slow pull. That wasn't working. She was tempted to ask Winnie for Vaseline, but surely that would ruin the dress even if it did help her get it up past her thighs. She tried jumping. Didn't Beyoncé say it made it easier to get jeans on if you jumped? Surely the same applied to dresses. She jumped up and down several times, but still, the dress didn't budge. The only thing that could get her into the dress now was prayer.

"This ain't my fault. This is so not my fault. This is all Sariah's doing. Please help me get into this dress."

"Did you say something, hun?"

"Uh, no. I'll be out in a sec." *But it probably won't be with the dress on…*

Deja made one more attempt to pull up the dress and, as if by a miracle, the seam popped just enough for her to inch the dress further up her thighs. You couldn't even tell where it had ripped – another miracle – but she would have to tell Winnie so she could repair it. If Sariah knew, she'd lose her mind.

Deja pulled the dress all the way up, forced her arms in the tight lacey sleeves, and mumbled, "I look ridiculous. Absolutely, one-hundred percent ridiculous."

There was no use in trying to zip the thing up on her own. At this point, it was impossible.

Finally stepping out, she said, "Winnie, I got it on," feeling her stomach cinch behind the uncomfortable fabric, and that's *after* she sucked it in a little.

"How beautiful," Winnie said, bringing her hands to a clap.

"Full disclosure—I heard something rip."

"Oh, I'm sure it's fine."

Deja walked to the showroom, stood on the pedestal, and looked at herself in the mirrors bordering the room. "Wow! This is a beautiful dress. I see why Sariah chose this one. Let me call her." Deja stepped down, grabbed her phone and called Sariah on video chat. Winnie positioned the phone far enough back so Sariah could see the full length of the dress while Deja returned to the pedestal.

When Sariah answered the video, she immediately gasped, saying, "Oh my goodness! I look so friggin' good."

"You mean *I* look good," Deja said, correcting

her.

"Yeah, whatever. You know what I meant."

"Hi, Sariah. I'm Winnie. It's nice to meet you. Would've been better if you were here."

"Yeah, I know. I got tied up at work."

Winnie said, "Okay, hang on a sec…I still have to zip up the dress so you can get an accurate visual."

"I think it's in everyone's best interest to leave that zipper alone, Winnie. I'm barely breathing right now. I'll probably be gasping for air if you zip me."

Winnie laughed and said, "I don't think so. We have plenty of room." She pulled the zipper up, and when it wouldn't zip up any further, she said, "Uh oh."

Deja cackled. "I told you not to—"

Deja stopped talking when she watched Dare walk inside.

Dare? What was he doing here? She was expecting Kris, who had yet to show up (thank goodness), but not Dare.

At the angle Dare entered, Sariah couldn't see him on video. Deja wouldn't have heard the last of it if Sariah knew Dare was there.

Winnie said, "Sweet mercy to life…is he the groom?"

"Shh," Deja said, quieting Winnie. She didn't want to alarm Sariah in any way.

"What's going on?" Sariah asked. "Is something wrong?"

"No. Nothing's wrong, Sariah. Winnie is trying to zip me up."

"I'm-a-trying," Winnie said, putting her all into it. The zipper wouldn't move up any further. "Now, hun," she whispered. "If I'm gon' get this thing zipped up, I'ma need you to suck it in a bit."

"I sucked it in ten minutes ago and never let it back out." Deja giggled, glancing at Dare.

Sariah didn't find anything funny. "What the heck, Deja? What did you do? Pig out last night and now you can't fit it?"

"No, I ate two baby carrots and had a sip of water last night, Sariah."

Dare shook his head. She really *did* eat carrots for dinner last night.

"Well, tap into the powers within. I need that dress zipped up."

"Sariah, you sound real silly right now."

"Why don't you focus so Winnie can get the dress zipped up?"

"You have a general idea of how it looks without it being zipped all the way up. Besides, it's your fault for ordering a size eight when you're a solid ten."

"Wait…" Winnie said excitingly. "I think I'm on to something. Just one…more…tug…and…voila! Houston, we're zipped!"

"Are you happy now, Sariah?" Deja asked. "Jeez! Got me standing up here looking like a busted can of biscuits."

"Thank you for getting it zipped, Winnie," Sariah said. "Now, I can see how it flatters my shape."

Deja said, "Yeah, she can see how it flatters *her* shape, but I'm the one who's shrink-wrapped right now. Even my toes hurt and I'm not even wearing shoes."

Dare looked down at her feet, but the gown was so long, he couldn't see them.

"Aw...this looks so good!" Sariah said. "Spin around, Deja."

"I would, but I can't move or breathe."

"I'll hold your hand," Winnie offered, then helped Deja rotate so Sariah could see the back of the gown.

"Perfect! Oh goody. I'm so happy! I knew this was the dress for me when I first saw it...just like I knew Kris was the one."

Deja's eyes rolled around several times, but she bit her tongue from rattling off an insult about Kris. That was getting old, and she was trying to be over it, but it was a struggle.

Meanwhile, Dare couldn't take his eyes off of Deja. When he first walked in, seeing her standing there in that gown sent a punch to his gut – that's how gorgeous she looked. He liked seeing her up on the pedestal in a white dress that looked like whipped cream against her chocolate skin. It was like she was on display for his eyes only. He took in her hourglass figure. He couldn't see those lovely curves of hers beneath the winter clothes she wore, but now, she was on full display to his delight. Skip all the nonsense about her body being too thick for the dress. She looked fine, and a little thickness ain't never hurt nobody, especially when that thickness fell in all the right places like her thighs and hips. She filled the dress beautifully. Every piece of lace, even the low-cut back gave her an elegant glow. He could imagine her hair in curls, hanging around her shoulders, bringing out the depth of her eyes.

The last time he'd seen a woman in a wedding gown was at his own wedding. While he wanted to forget about it, the image of Heather walking down the aisle was burned into his memory. He wished he could remove it. If he could, the transition from married to divorced would've been a lot smoother. Marriage was forever for *him*, but for Heather, it had been the opposite.

"Okay, then, am I done now?" Deja asked. "I need to get this thing off of me before this zipper puts somebody's eye out."

"Ugh…why do you have to be so extra, Deja?"

"Why do you have to be so *bleh*, Sariah?"

"You wish you could be half of that."

"I don't want to be half of that. I don't want to be *any* of that."

"Yeah, whatever. When you get back, why don't you look into an exercise regimen? There's no way you shouldn't fit that dress perfectly."

"You do know it's a size eight, right?"

"Uh…yeah!"

"But you're not an eight."

"So what? I can still fit it. Anywho, I gotta run. Toodles." She hung up, ending the video call.

"Ugh…why me?" Deja said quietly.

"Don't listen to her. I think you look beautiful," Dare spoke up to say.

Deja glanced over at him. "Don't lie."

"I'm serious. You do. You look like a princess."

"No, I don't. I'ma tell you what I look like. You know those vacuum-sealed bags that you can put a pillow in and suck all the air out to save space for storage?"

Dare chuckled.

"*That's* what I look like."

"You don't. Why are you so hard on yourself?"

She shrugged. "Because I can be…and I'm not *perfect*…like her."

"Your sister?"

"Yep. She's two years younger than I am, and I've always watched her do whatever she wanted and accomplish anything she set out to do."

"You can do the same, but you don't have to be like her. You're you. You're fine just the way you are."

"Thanks for saying that. It's—"

"Hey, holler when you're ready to take that off, hun," Winnie said, interrupting their conversation.

"Okay. Thank you, Winnie."

Deja looked at Dare and continued, "I know you didn't show up here to listen to me whine about my sister. Why are you here? Did Kris send you?"

"No. I'm still on the clock. I knew you'd be here today, and I wanted to apologize to you."

"For what? Ducking away from me when I tried to kiss you on the cheek last night?"

"Yeah. I—"

"You didn't have to take time out of your day to come over here and apologize to me for that, Dare."

"I did. I was rude and—"

"No. *I* was rude. I always get too comfortable with people. I shouldn't have. I mean, I should've known a man like you had a girlfriend."

"I don't have a girlfriend."

"Okay, then. A *potential* girlfriend?" she asked, narrowing her eyes.

"What are you talking about?"

"When we were out to dinner the other night, a woman called you."

"Yes. Jolene, my housekeeper."

Ah...his housekeeper, she said to herself. So, why did he dodge her kiss if there was no woman in his life? She told him, "Well, I shouldn't have tried to kiss you, but it's all good. If you would excuse me, I have to peel this dress off. The lace is digging into my skin."

"Okay," Dare said, standing. "Hey, um…"

"What's up?" she asked, staring up at him. He looked conflicted like he wanted to ask her something, or offer an explanation for last night, but he wasn't saying a word.

After a few moments, he said, "It's nothing. Bye, Deja."

"Bye, Dare."

He rubbed his hands down the pant legs of his jeans and headed out.

* * *

"SARIAH TOLD ME the dress looked nice," Justine said.

Deja fell across the bed with the phone on speaker. She could hear the delight in her mother's tone. She responded, "So, you agree with her having *me* try the dress on?"

"Why wouldn't you, Deja? Sariah was in a bind. You're her maid of honor. Her sister. She had to do what she had to do. I'm sure you would've done the same thing if you felt like you couldn't be there, correct?"

"No. I would've rescheduled at a time more convenient, so I could try on my *own* dress. And do you really think if the situation was reversed, and I was the one getting married, Sariah would drop everything she's doing to drive like four hours away to taste some cakes and try on a wedding gown for me?"

"I think she would have, but of course, we don't have to worry about that. You haven't been on a date since that bobble-headed boy you went to prom with in high school. Besides, you have the kind of job where you can leave at any given time. Sariah doesn't have the same flexibility."

Deja wanted to scream. It was no surprise that her mother had a favorite, and it wasn't her. She said, "Ma, let's talk about something else besides Sariah. How are you and dad doing?"

"We're doing fine. We've been making sure people RSVP for the reception."

And they were right back to the wedding...

"That's awesome. Listen, I have to go find something for dinner. I had a rough day."

Justine giggled. "Really, dear. You tried on *one* wedding dress."

"And that proved to be taxing enough. I burned five hundred calories trying to take the thing off."

"You should've enjoyed the experience. Hopefully, it'll give you a feeling of wanting to get married soon."

Deja sat straight up on the bed, "Wow. On that note, I'm going to go ahead and hang up."

Deja ended the call, placing the phone on the nightstand. Then she headed to the kitchen grumbling saying, "Letting my chicken get cold talking to you 'bout some nonsense. I'll be glad when this wedding is over."

She took her dinner to the living room and turned up the volume on the TV.

"Mmm," she moaned. "So much better than those nasty carrots I had last night...to try on a dress...for my ungrateful sister. I sacrificed dinner for her. Dinner! Does anyone appreciate what I do? No! Nobody!"

A tap at the door jolted her. She got up from the sofa and walked to the door, peering through the peephole. To her surprise, Dare was standing there. That made two times he'd popped up unannounced.

She opened the door and asked, "Dare...what are you doing here?"

"I was wondering if you had a minute to talk." He looked at her cheek. It was filled with something. He looked at her hand and saw a chicken leg. He grinned. "Wait...I feel like I'm interrupting something."

Deja looked at the drumstick in her hand and said, "No, you're not. Come on in." She pushed the door open wider so he could enter. "I bought a bucket of chicken."

Dare stood by the door and stomped snow off of his boots before he proceeded any further. "A bucket? Were you expecting company?"

"Not at all. I figured since I starved myself yesterday, I had some making up to do today. It's all protein, right? Protein is good for you."

"Yes it is, but too many calories are not," he said, sitting on the loveseat in the living room.

"Then help yourself to some, Mr. Stokes. You look like you just got off of work. I know you haven't eaten anything."

"I haven't, but I don't want to interrupt your food fest."

"Nonsense. I'll make you a plate."

"Okay…" Dare said although he didn't come by to eat, but since she was offering he accepted.

"Here you are," she said, handing him a ceramic plate from the stash of dishes in the cupboard that the resort supplied.

"Thank you," he said.

"You're welcome," she responded, sitting on the sofa.

He reached for a thigh first, taking a hearty bite. "That's good chicken," he said, mumbling as he chewed.

"Ain't it?" Deja sipped tea, then asked, "So, what's on your mind?"

"I wanted to share something with you about me. I have my reasons for being who I am."

"I'm listening."

"I was married for ten years. We were happy. Well, I guess *she* wasn't all that happy since she's the one who left me."

"That's terrible," Deja said. She didn't want to get all in his business, but she had plenty of questions. She hoped he'd cover them all without her having to ask.

Dare continued, "She would say some of the same things Kris says about me—I'm boring.

That's what she told me. Like, straight up. I know I'm not the most exciting person around, but there's more to a relationship than that. We made a vow, a commitment to each other. How can a woman break that vow because she thinks I'm boring?"

"I don't know. I can't answer on her behalf and I don't know you well enough to comment on what happened. What I will say is—I think you're exciting. You took me death tubing—I mean *snow* tubing. That was fun."

He chuckled. "Yeah it was, but I guess it was too little, too late to save my marriage."

"You want to work it out with her, I assume."

"No, I don't. We've been divorced for six years now."

"Oh. So, you've moved on?"

"Not really." Dare sighed inwardly.

"I'm sorry if it feels like I'm prying. I just—"

"No, you're fine, Deja. I brought this to you, so you have a right to ask anything you want."

Deja set her plate on the coffee table and told him, "Sometimes, people change. What they thought they wanted initially sometimes wears off, or they grow out of it."

"Do you think it's okay to leave a marriage when a spouse doesn't meet the *new* expectations of the other person?"

"Absolutely not. I wouldn't do that. If I thought the relationship needed a little something extra, I'd make suggestions. I'm not the one to be on the prowl looking for another man because I'm bored. But that's just me. I can't speak for other women."

Deja watched as Dare set his plate on the table and said, "Let me grab you some water."

She filled a glass with ice, cracked open a bottle of water, and poured it over the ice before handing it to him.

"Thank you."

"You're welcome."

"So," she said, sitting on the sofa again folding her left leg beneath her. "Have you been involved with anyone since the divorce?"

"No," Dare responded after a long sip of water.

His answer made her think about what Sariah had told her – that Dare was a little 'messed up' after the end of his marriage, and she was starting to have her opinions about it. Six years was a long time to go without dating, well for a man at least. She never dated. She worked. They were the same in that respect, weren't they? How could she judge him when she didn't date either? That didn't mean anything was wrong with her, so why did it have to mean something was wrong with him?

Ugh, Sariah, get out of my head with this nonsense of yours!

"Why don't you date?" Deja decided to ask instead of coming to her own conclusions about the situation.

"I lost faith in relationships. After what went down with my ex-wife, I can't see myself trusting anyone."

"Never?"

"I don't want to say never, but it'll definitely be a challenge. What about you?"

"What about me?" she asked, searching through the bucket of chicken, looking for a wing.

"You're enjoying that chicken a little too much."

"I am, but do you blame me after those carrots?"

"No. Not at all. Eat up."

Dare took a sip of water, then leaned back on the sofa, watching Deja eat like she hadn't eaten in weeks. He asked, "Why don't you date?"

"Who said I didn't?" she asked, looking at him.

"Just a hunch."

She shrugged. "Wow. It's that obvious. Okay…I don't know. I guess I don't make the time. Or I keep thinking I'll meet someone by some serendipitous chance meeting or something—you know—like in the movies."

"Sort of like a woman stranded in a snowstorm and this guy stops to help her—that kind of unexpected meeting?"

She beamed. "Yeah. Like that."

Dare drank more water then asked, "How has your vacation been so far?"

"Good, and it's all because of you."

"Nah. Don't give me credit for that."

"It's true. I broke down, you rescued me. You saved me from having to be alone with your brother. *Ugh.* Please, tell me—how are you two even related?"

Dare fell back laughing. "I could ask you the same thing about Sariah, and I've never met her."

"Right."

"But Kris—he's a typical people pleaser. He's always had this desire to be the best, even if it meant making others feel like they're not on his level. I know I make more money than him and honestly, I'm more successful than he is, but I'm not the kind of person to rub my success in anyone's face. I like what I do. I don't do it to be better than anyone. I do it because I love doing it."

"What made you get into building houses?"

"I always considered myself a builder. I took all the shop classes in high school and when I was a teenager, I built a doghouse for our Labrador. I didn't use a plan or anything—just right off the top of my head. A few years after I got my official builder's license, I built an addition onto my parent's home."

"Really?"

"Yes. My mother wanted a bigger master and walk-in closet. So, I made that happen for her."

"Did you build your house?"

Dare smirked, but sadness crept into his heart. "I did," he responded and left it at that.

Deja said, "I feel like I hit a nerve or something."

He noted her discernment and said, "I built it for my family—a family I never had and probably never will have." Dare rubbed his hands together and stood up. This wasn't a subject he wanted to get into, so he decided leaving would be best.

"Leaving so soon?"

"Yeah."

"Oh. I'm sorry. I know I haven't been much company."

"You have," he told her. "Thank you for dinner."

Deja stood up to join him. "You're welcome."

"So, I'll be seeing you, I guess."

"Yeah. I'm sure we'll bump into each other again. Oh, I'm going to—wait. Never mind."

"What is it?"

"Nothing. I was going to invite you somewhere with me, then remembered that you're working. *I'm* the one on vacation. Sort of."

"Where are you going?"

"A client of mine told me about this place called The Apple House. She said I *had* to go there like it was non-negotiable, so I was thinking of heading that way tomorrow."

"You should. I don't know why I didn't think to tell you about that. It's a nice place."

"Okay, then. Can you come with me?" she asked. "Just for like an hour or so."

"What time are you trying to go?"

"Around one."

"I can do that. I'll meet you there at one, then go straight back to work when I leave."

"Sounds like a date—I mean—plan."

"Yeah."

"Alright, then. Goodnight," she said, purposely taking a step back from him to avoid kissing him again. The last time, it didn't go too well.

"You don't have to do that, Deja."

"I don't want to make you feel uncomfortable."

"You're not." He took a step back over to her, closing the space between them, and pressed his lips to her temple. Then he said, "Goodnight, Deja."

"Goodnight, Dare."

He walked over to the door, pulled the handle, and said, "Don't eat the rest of that chicken."

A blustery laugh charged out of her. "I won't."

"Bye," he said, stepping outside. "See ya tomorrow."

"Bye."

She waited until he reached the truck, waved a final time then closed the door, doing a happy dance. Something about Dare excited her, especially the kiss. His lips pressed against her temple felt like he'd left a permanent impression there. Was this the giddy excitement people felt when they met someone who was date-worthy? She could get used to this feeling, especially with a man like him. He was handsome and charming – as far as she was concerned, the complete package. But Dare had layers to him that he kept under wraps. And now she hated the fact he had trust issues – that some woman had used and abused his heart. If only she'd found him first…

CHAPTER 9

"THESE HAVE GOT to be the best donuts I've had in my life!" Deja said, then stuffed her mouth with another hearty bite.

Dare smiled as he watched her devour them. "And to think you were reluctant to try them."

"Yes, I was skeptical. I've never had apple butter donuts. Now that I know better, I'm taking some of these babies home and by *some*, I mean like three dozen."

Deja looked on as Dare took a bite of the donut. As she watched him chew, she wasn't sure if it was the donut causing her mouth to water or him. It was probably his lips – the sweet goodness she remembered pressed to her temple last night – sweeter than those donuts she was cramming down her throat. Every time she was near him, his presence usurped hers. Was that the testosterone or his aura? How did a man like him let a woman derail his plans for his life? Handsomeness oozed from him at every angle, but what she couldn't see — what *really* counted — was his heart. It was damaged, and that was a blow he had yet to recover from.

"Chase your donuts with a shot of cider," he suggested.

"Oh, that's how y'all get down in the valley? Alright, I'm game."

Dare handed her a mug of hot cider. She took a long sip and pinched her eyelids together as if she'd tossed back a shot of tequila. She was bracing herself because she'd never had cider before, but if this trip taught her nothing else, it gave her a lesson on the adventure she could have by trying new things. So, she tried it. And she liked it.

"How is it?" Dare inquired.

"It's delicious!" she marveled. "Tastes like my hopes and dreams."

"Then why'd you ball your face up?" he asked, amused.

"I was bracing myself in case it was nasty."

"Ah…gotcha."

"Dare? Is that you?"

Dare and Deja turned to the sound of the woman's voice calling his name. Dare frowned a little, Deja noticed, then she studied the beautiful brown-skinned woman as she smiled, bouncing a toddler on her hip.

"I thought that was you," the woman said, excitement in her voice and features. "How have you been? You look good."

Deja looked at Dare when he seemed to have frozen in place. He wasn't saying a word. He blinked and looked down at the mug in his hand like he didn't want to say a word at first, then finally responded saying, "I'm good."

He immediately turned to walk in the opposite direction, away from the woman when she asked, "Aren't you going to introduce me to your friend?"

The woman set her eyes on Deja. Deja looked at Dare, spotting a more prominent version of the frown he'd had on his face before. Who was this woman who had him frowning?

It wasn't...*her*...was it? The woman who'd broken his heart? His ex-wife?

It couldn't be...

Dare cleared his throat. He would've never thought he'd run into his ex-wife here of all places, especially on a weekday, but there she was holding her daughter. He'd heard she had a little girl, and now he was seeing that for himself.

Standing there, all he could think about was the heartache she'd caused him and now she was wanted introductions? For what purpose?

"No, that's not necessary, Heather," he told her. What was it to her who he was with? It wasn't any of her business.

Dare attempted to walk away again and heard Heather's voice once more when she said, "You're a good man, Dare. Don't ever forget that."

Dare told himself to walk away, but her words tore into him. He turned around, looked at Heather and said, "I must not be that good of a man. I couldn't keep you."

Heather sighed. "That's neither here nor there, Dare. I just—I was hoping we could be cordial. It shouldn't be so awkward when we see each other."

Dare stifled a bitter laugh. "So, the cheater wants to set expectations. How exactly does that work?"

Feeling like she was witnessing something she shouldn't have been witnessing, Deja walked away. The conversation between Dare and Heather was teetering toward an argument and honestly, none of this was any of her business. She stepped behind a greeting card rack and pretended to be looking at them, but she was still in earshot of Dare and his ex-wife.

Heather said, "I'm bringing it up because it's been years, Dare. I see you're with someone here, but I heard you were still single and I—"

"How do you know what I am?"

"People talk."

"Yes, they do. They certainly had a lot to say about you."

"Listen, Dare. I don't want to argue with you. I want you to be happy. I really do. And I think we could eventually be friends again. We used to be the best of friends."

"You walked out on me, on *us*, on *our*

marriage! The ink on the divorce papers wasn't even dry before you'd already started planning your new life with that man. So, live your life, Heather…with your kids…and whoever else, but don't count on me ever being a part of it."

"Is he bothering you, sweetheart?" Heather's husband, Chase, walked up asking, throwing his arm around her.

Dare flashed an angry smirk. Not only was he face-to-face with his ex-wife – the woman he used to love – but her new husband was standing next to her with his arms around her, being territorial like he *had* to protect Heather and his child against Dare. And to think Chase was once his best friend…

Dare shook his head and said, "I don't need this. And, to answer your question, I don't care how many years have passed, Heather. We will *never* be friends and things will always be awkward whenever we run into each other. What did you expect? That we'd all hold hands, roast marshmallows and sing kumbaya after you left me for who I thought was my best friend?"

Chase stepped forward and said, "Ay, man. It's been years. You still sound bitter. You should be over it by now."

It took all the willpower Dare had to turn away from Chase. If he hadn't, there would've been an all-out brawl right there in the store. People were already taking out their cell phones either to record or call the police as he was heading for the exit.

Deja stood dazed for a moment, in disbelief that all of this was going down on her last full day in the valley, but she was more bothered by the circumstances. Dare hadn't told her the man Heather had left him for was his best friend. That meant he'd been betrayed not once, but twice – both times by people he once trusted.

When Deja came out of her daze, she caught up to Dare in the parking lot. He was about to climb up into his truck.

"Dare, wait."

He stopped right before opening the door and said, "I apologize, Deja. You shouldn't have seen any of that."

"It's okay. I understand—"

"No," he said, interrupting her. "It's not okay. You didn't come here for this and I have to get back to work. Honestly, that's where I should've been all along. If I hadn't come here, I wouldn't have run into them."

"You're probably right," Deja said, feeling like this was her fault now. "You would've run into them somewhere, eventually. Don't you think you need to face this, or at the very least forgive her so you can finally be free and move on?"

"I wouldn't expect you to understand my pain, Deja. You've never been in love. You don't know what it's like to give someone your all, only to have them trample all over you, so no, I can't forgive her. She ruined my life. I hope you enjoy the rest of your vacation."

Dare started the truck and drove away.

Deja watched as his truck got further and further away until he was out of sight. The last few minutes were intense for her, so she could only imagine how he must've felt carrying the weight of so much duplicity. This must've been his reaction every time he saw his ex. He hadn't moved on and no doubt it was the circumstances. Heather left him for his best friend. Talk about betrayal…this had to rank near the top. While heartbreak didn't have an expiration date, she didn't like how he was torturing himself.

That's why forgiveness was so important. Forgiveness was more for the person who was wronged – not the person who wronged you. When you forgave someone, no matter how badly they hurt you, it took the hurt, the burden and the suppressed anger away from you – away from your spirit. When that forgiveness didn't happen, you kept all the anger and bitterness bottled up which, in turn, made you stagnant – unable to move on with life because of the grudge you're holding on to. In the end, you only ended up hurting yourself and to a greater degree than the offender. That's what Dare was doing – hurting himself worse than what Heather and Chase had done to him.

It was time for him to let that drama go. She knew that and she'd only known about his situation for a few days. So, why was it so hard for him to realize that holding on to this was destroying him? It was messing with his mind, interfering with his peace, and greatly disrupting his life.

CHAPTER 10

<DING DONG>

The chime of the doorbell forced Dare's eyes open. After work, he crashed on the sofa with no intention of doing anything else for the rest of the day, especially after that run-in with Heather and Chase. So who was ringing his doorbell at 7:00 p.m. on a Friday?

<Ding dong>

"Be right there."

He opened the door and there stood his parents with Kris standing behind them. They all had a dish in their hands, wrapped in aluminum foil.

"Surprise," his mother, Carmen, said jovially, a beanie covering her blonde hair. "We got food, and you can thank us later for saving you from another lonely Friday night at home."

"Lonely Friday night," Dare said evenly.

"Exactly," Kris said, walking past his brother. "We got your back, bruh."

"I wasn't on board with this, son," his father said, shaking his head. "They forced me to join in with the shenanigans."

"It's all good, Dad," Dare said, patting him on the shoulder.

Dare closed the door, shutting out the cold air that tried to follow them inside.

They set up shop in the dining room. Carmen moseyed on to the kitchen to get plates and silverware. When Dare stepped inside, she asked him, "Do you have some bread around here somewhere?"

"No. I don't eat a lot of bread."

"I knew it. I told your father we should've stopped for bread. You can hardly keep food in this house now that there's no woman in here making sure everything is running like it is supposed to."

His mother was yet again dropping hints – making him aware of his single status and if he was somehow *unaware*. As he'd always done, he dismissed it. His mother knew Jolene did his shopping and house cleaning. He was getting along fine without a wife. He returned to the dining room with plates.

Their father prayed over the food, then Carmen said, "Okay, Dare, why don't you get first dibs. It's been a while since you've had a good home-cooked meal, I'm sure."

Another jab…and it wasn't helping matters that Kris was enjoying every second of it. Why wouldn't he? He was their golden child – the one who was getting married in a few weeks – not the one whose life was turned upside down due to no fault of his own.

Dare took a piece of roasted chicken and mashed potatoes. His mother made the best homemade potatoes. Succotash was the third element of their impromptu dinner and Dare knew it would be a challenge to focus on enjoying this time with his parents without his personal life coming into play. His mother was already coming out swinging.

"So, Kris told us you weren't going to be his best man, Dare," Carmen said. "I want to know why? Is it a jealousy thing, because you can find yourself a nice girl if you'd just open your eyes? Women have been throwing themselves at you the moment Heather left this house."

Dare glanced up at his mother and said, "No, I'm not the best man. Kris didn't *ask* me to be his best man." Dare chose to ignore the rest of what she'd said. He wasn't about to entertain any woman chasing after him just to fill a vacancy in his life.

"I didn't think I had to ask you to be my best man," Kris spat out from across the table. "When you and Heather got married, I was *your* best man, so I thought it was a given you'd be mine. Since you didn't volunteer or even hint that you wanted to be a part of my wedding, I asked Nicholas to do it."

Dare tried to force himself to eat so no one, his mother in particular, would think anything was wrong. But there was something wrong. He didn't like this. Something about his family barging in on him, in such bad weather especially, didn't feel right, and he wasn't up for company. He definitely didn't want to hear anything about marriage – not Kris', his old one to Heather or the possibility of a new one.

"Don't tell me you're not going to be in your brother's wedding," his mother said.

"I didn't say that."

"And you didn't say you would either," Kris said.

Dare said, "You know I have a lot going on with the new subdivision and all—"

"Dare!" Carmen said, looking at her oldest son like the end of the world was imminent.

"It's cool, Ma," Kris said. "Why would he want to see *me* happy and married?"

"Kris, I want nothing but the best for you," Dare said truthfully.

"Yeah, I can't tell…" Kris murmured.

Dare sighed internally and made himself eat.

Carmen said, "You know what? I'm just gon' say it. I'm getting concerned about you being over here in this big ol' house by yourself. It's been six years since Heather—"

"Carmen…" Kevin said, trying to stop her from going on a rant. He knew his wife had genuine concerns about their son. She talked about Dare incessantly, like he couldn't make it on his own without having a woman around. She knew he was capable, but she wanted Kris to have a good woman by his side – a woman he could build a future with – but if Dare needed time, Kevin wasn't about to force his son to make a move.

Kevin said, "Honey, I thought we were here to enjoy dinner. Let's not badger Dare with questions."

"It's not badgering, Dad," Kris said as if he was defending his mother. "I think it needs to be said." He looked at Dare and continued, "It's kinda sad how you let one person throw off the trajectory of your whole life. It's like, get over it already and quit with the broken-hearted act."

Dare had heard enough. He pushed his plate away and closed his eyes. With his elbows on the table, he brought his hands to a steeple and folded his hands together. He could usually brush off the sly remarks of his family, but he wasn't having it today. Not after the run-in with Heather and Chase. Not after he ditched Deja. Not after his folks showed up here unannounced without even giving him a courtesy call. No, he was done with it – *all* of it.

When he opened his eyes, he asked calmly, "How many times have you been married, Kris?"

"I've never been married. You know that."

"And you've never been in a serious relationship before you met Sariah. So, how could

129

you *possibly* know the mental torture and anguish that happens to a person when a spouse—a person who was supposed to be your life partner—betrays your marriage vows? This is not some minor incident. I'm not just supposed to *get over* it. Heather was my *wife*, the woman who was slated to be the mother of my children. I built this house for us…built this house for the family I'll never have. You have no idea—*no idea*—what that did to me. I don't think any of you do, so let me tell you. Let me tell what happened when my wife told me, by her actions that, I wasn't enough. It destroyed me. Everything I've worked for, everything I wanted in life was ripped away from me and now, at forty-one years old, what do I have to show for myself? Nothing. I have nothing. No wife, no children, no nothing! And all everyone wants to do is badger me constantly about what I *don't* have. My life isn't a reality TV show where you all sit back and comment like I'm not here. I'm here. I'm living this nightmare. The only thing that's keeping me from throwing in the towel is construction. Trust me, I've thought about ending it all after the divorce. If I'm not alive, I can't feel anything, right? I'd be free. I wouldn't have to put up with the constant disrespect from none of you about this situation. *Dare, you need a woman…Dare, you need to get over it already…Dare, somebody needs to fix you a home-cooked meal.* Tell you what…have someone rip your heart out of your chest and see how fast you're able to get over it?"

Dare pushed away from the table and went outside, standing on the snow-covered deck trying to blow off some steam. He was so heated, the thirty-six-degree temperature didn't bother him in the least. He exhaled, seeing his own breath appear before him. It wasn't long before he heard someone coming outside. He didn't turn around to see who it was before he said, "Don't bother."

"Son, I wanted to make sure you were okay."

Dare turned to look at his father. One thing his father never did was burden him with questions about his situation, or when he would marry again. He gave him space. He wished his mother and Kris extended him the same courtesy.

"Are you okay?" Kevin asked.

"I don't know what I am, Dad."

His father said, "Ah…you'll be alright, son. You know me…I don't try to get all in your business, and I don't like how Kris and your mother are always on your back about Heather, and I *told* them that. I wanted to come out here and let you know that it's not over. Your life isn't over by any means. You're still young. You have a lot more living to do, Dare."

Dare didn't say a word at first. He crossed his arms and only stared back at his father. Biting back his emotions, he said, "I feel like a failure."

"You're not a failure. You did nothing wrong. *You* were the one who was betrayed. Not once, but twice! You can't blame yourself for someone else's actions."

"I know." Dare sighed. "I ran into them today."

"Who?"

"Heather, Chase, and *their* daughter. The things that crossed my mind should never cross anyone's mind. I just…I don't know. It was like a slap in the face. Without saying a word, she basically said, 'you weren't good enough for me, so I'm with him now'."

"Correction—a woman like that who turned on you wasn't good enough for you from the start. It took years for you to see it, and for *her* to realize it. Dare, your life isn't over because you had some people who betrayed you. I know you want children and you still have a family, son. Nothing's over. You can still have a family. You can have all the children you want. In fact, everything you want is there for the taking, but you have to be willing to take it. Let go of the past before it ruins your future. Give yourself permission to love again. Now, that's all I'm going to say about it. I'm not going to badger you. Just think about it."

"You're right," Dare said. "Everything you said is right."

"What do you think you should do about it? I mean, honestly, when was the last time you went out and had yourself a good time?"

He didn't have to go back far to figure that

out. He'd had plenty of laughs with Deja and he hadn't known her for a full week. A small smile came to his face when he thought about how Deja had stuffed herself with donuts and was chowing down on a bucket of chicken all by herself before he had shown up. She was beautiful in every way – a woman who raised his curiosity.

He told his father, "It's nerve-racking to start over."

"It is. It's a risk, but you don't know how great your life could be if you don't try. Look at how much you've already overcome. You need to try. And in the meantime, I'll talk to your mom about getting off your back a little."

"Thanks, Dad. I appreciate it."

"All right…let's get back inside where it's warm. It feels like Iceland out here."

Dare chuckled. "Yeah, it does."

As they stepped back inside, Dare noticed Kris standing in the kitchen holding a beer.

Sensing Kris wanted to speak with his brother privately, Kevin said, "I'll be in the dining room."

As their father exited, Kris said, "Look, man— I give you grief sometimes because I hope it will shake you out of whatever it is you're going through. I know it's been hard, but I had no idea how hard it has been for you and I want to apologize for being insensitive to your situation. You're right. I don't know how it feels to be betrayed in that matter, and I don't know what I would do if that happened to me. So, I'm sorry."

"It's all good, Kris. Don't worry about it."

"No, it's not all good."

"I would've never thought you'd be sitting over here thinking about ending it all." Kris shook his head. "You're my big brother. I couldn't imagine my life without you, bruh."

Kris walked over to Dare and engulfed him in a big, manly bear hug.

Dare wiggled his way free and said, "Hey, chill with all that, Kris. I'm fine."

"Are you sure because you say things like that, but you'll be thinking something else totally different?"

"Yeah. I'm good."

"If you ever feel like you need to talk, let me know."

"I will, Kris."

"I mean it, Dare."

"Okay, I hear you."

"And I would like for you to be my best man. With the situation with Heather and all, I wasn't sure how'd you'd feel about it. That's why I didn't ask."

"Sure. I'll be your best man."

Excited, Kris was approaching his brother with his arms spread open wide, seeking a second hug.

Dare, knowing how extra his brother could be, said, "No more hugs tonight, Kris."

"Okay. Fine. No hugs, but we need to get you

fitted for a tux. The wedding is right around the corner. What does your schedule look like tomorrow?"

"I can make some time in the morning. Let me know where to meet you."

"You got it," Kris said, patting Dare on the shoulder. "Isn't that weird how everything works out. You're my best man. Deja is the maid-of-honor. You'll be walking her down the aisle, which I'm sure you don't mind since you two seem to have hit it off."

Dare instantly thought about how beautiful Deja looked in the wedding gown. He could only imagine how beautiful she looked in her bridesmaid dress, and he was thrilled to be the man to walk with her.

"Yeah, that will be nice," Dare replied. "She's a good woman."

"Sorry to interrupt," their mother said, stepping into the kitchen, "But it's my turn."

Kris returned to the dining room and Carmen walked up to Dare and embraced him. She reached up to place her hands on his face and said, "You know I love you."

"I love you too, Mother."

Tears welled up in her eyes. She said, "I only want the best for you, my dear son."

His heart ached as he witnessed the sadness on her face. "I know you do, Mother, but I need you to know I'll be fine. I don't want you, Dad or Kris worrying about me. I have my moments, but

I'm ready to get my life back on track. It only took Dad to remind me that I'm not *old.*"

She chuckled softly and said, "No, you're not old. You're my amazing, talented firstborn son, and I want you to have everything your heart desires. That's my hope for you and your brother."

Dare held his mother's delicate hands and said, "I need you to be patient while I'm working hard to obtain that—on my own schedule."

"I will. From this point forward, I'll leave you alone about finding this and that. If I get out of line, tell me to hush."

"You know I can't do that to you," he said, holding his mother in his arms and embracing her warmly. He was grateful for his family – that everyone had come to an understanding. He even came to his own conclusions. He had been holding back, living in the shadows. With so many people rooting for him, there was no need for that. He had to get out there and go for it. He had to start living life.

CHAPTER 11

DEJA HAD PACKED up her clothes last night, but this morning, she realized how much she'd settled into the condo. She had stuff everywhere. Takeout containers, plastic spoons and forks littered the dining room table. Snacks and other food items were all over the counter. She bagged up the food and carried the bags to the car.

After pulling her suitcase outside through the fresh snow, securing it in the trunk, she did a final walkthrough of the place to make sure she had all of her belongings. Walking past the bathroom in the hallway, she saw the large Jacuzzi. She never got a chance to enjoy it because her days were filled with taking care of Sariah's wedding needs or hanging out with Dare.

She thought about Dare several times as she packed her bags. Her heart went out to him after what happened Friday afternoon. They'd run into his ex, her husband and child. Dare did the mature thing by removing himself from the situation, but that also meant he had to remove himself from her in the process.

She didn't like that. She enjoyed spending time with him. Her days in the valley certainly wouldn't have been the same without him.

Standing in front of the condo, she took a deep breath and said, "Well, until next time…"

She got in the car, cranked it up and turned the heat to the highest setting, hoping the defrost function would help clear her windshield of snow and ice. So far, it wasn't helping. She turned on the radio in time to hear the local meteorologist give a weather update, stating that due to the twenty-nine-degree temperature and the fact that it had snowed yet again last night, most roads were impassable. He advised drivers to stay off the roads, especially the back roads and secondary streets, as these didn't get the same attention as the main roads and highways.

Deja froze.

Literally and mentally.

What was she going to do now that she had to check out of the condo? She knew this particular property only allowed lengthier stays – not one-night bookings. Now, she'd had to find a hotel. But could she drive to a hotel without sliding into a ditch or causing an accident? That was the question.

And Sariah strikes again…

She took out her cell phone and saw a missed call from a 540 number. Thinking it might've been Dare, she dialed the number back.

"Hey, girl…you're not leaving today, are you?"

She frowned. "Kris?"

"Yeah, it's me. Good morning."

"Ugh…" she said. If she knew it was him, she wouldn't have answered.

"Where are you calling me from?"

"My parent's house. Can you believe it? They're the only couple in the United States that still uses a landline." He grinned.

"Why didn't you call me on your cell phone?"

"I forgot to charge it last night. And, you probably wouldn't have answered had I called from my number."

You got that right!

"So, what do you want?"

"I was watching the news. They said the roads are impassable. Aren't you supposed to be checking out today?"

"I just did."

"Well, I'm over at my folks' place like I said. You're welcome to join us. I mean, you *are* going to be family soon."

"I'd rather eat orange peels than stay anywhere near you, Kris."

Kris grinned. "Everybody wants to be near me. I'm that cool."

"Maybe to Sariah you are…"

"Ay, we can talk about how much you adore me later. I was calling because I want you to stay off of these roads. It's bad out here, sis. I figure since you seem to be fond of my brother, why don't you stay over at his place for a day or so? I'm sure he won't mind."

"I can't do that, Kris. How would I look barging in on your brother like that? I hardly know him."

"You know him well enough."

"No, and don't bother Dare with this. I'll find a motel as soon as the layer of ice that's blanketing my windshield melts."

"You didn't scrape your windshield?"

"No. It's currently at ice-skating rink status. How do you scrape a sheet of ice? I thought about bamming it with a lug wrench I saw in my trunk."

"Don't you go *bamming* anything. Jeez! You're going to bust the glass. Do you need me to come over there?"

"No. By the time you get over here, it would have melted already."

"Well, let me know what you're going to do. I can get you a room if need be, but I think staying with my brother is the move for you. He could sure use the company."

"What?"

"Talk to ya later, Deja."

Kris had hung up without answering her question. How could he use the company? She wondered what that meant. Was Dare in a bad way after what had happened yesterday to the point he needed company to take his mind off of things?

Deja attempted to turn on her windshield wipers. Frozen in ice, the wipers didn't budge.

"Grrr," she growled. She got out of the car and slammed the door. The motion must've broken up the ice because some of it broke off. That must've meant the ice was soft enough now to where she could use an ice scraper. She took it from the trunk and cleared a spot on the windshield on the driver's side. The passenger side was still packed with snow and ice. The windshield wipers still wouldn't budge.

"This will have to do because it's too cold out here to be doing this mess. *Ugh*."

She tossed the scraper in the back seat and got back inside the car, rubbing her hands together. Before she could shift the car into drive, her phone was ringing. She recognized Dare's number immediately. After yesterday, she didn't think she'd hear from him again. She knew she'd see him at the wedding, but this phone call was quite the surprise.

"Hello."

"Hi, Deja. How are you this morning?"

"I'm frozen. How are you, Dare?"

A soft chuckle came through the line. He said, "I'm okay. I hear you're looking for a place to stay."

Deja sighed. "I told Kris not to bother you—"

"It's not a bother. Tell me what's going on?"

"I checked out of the resort today. I called the

reservation desk to see if I could stay a few extra days, but they are completely booked. I told Kris I'd get a hotel since the roads are impassible, but if I drive slowly, I can probably make it home."

"You shouldn't be driving in this. I have a five-bedroom house and, as you know, it's only me here, so—"

"I couldn't. I don't want to impose."

"If it was a problem, I would tell you."

"No, you wouldn't." *You're too nice of a guy.*

"Okay, you got me there," he admitted, "But it's not a problem. Really. Where are you now?"

"In my car, sitting outside of the condo waiting for the windshield to defrost." She tried the wiper blades again. Nothing.

"How about I come pick you up?"

"No. I think I'm going to try and make it home."

"Please don't do that. It's too dangerous out there. Not only do you have to be careful, but you'll have other people driving like maniacs. You'll have to watch out for them, too. I have plenty of room. I don't mind if you spend a day or two with me."

Deja thought about it for a moment. She was in a bind, and she didn't want to be stranded on the highway again. The safest option was to wait until the roads had cleared. She said, "Okay, I'll drive to your house. What's your address?"

"I'll text it to you, Deja, but I really wish you would let me come over there and pick you up. I heard the roads were horrible."

"It won't make much sense for both of us to be out here in this mess. I'll drive slow, and if I slide into a ditch somewhere, I'll call you to save me. Again."

He chuckled. "Okay. Deal. I just sent my address to you. Did you get it?"

"Um, lemme see," she said, holding the phone in front of the steering wheel so she could see the screen. "Yep. I got it. How long would a normal drive take from here to there?"

"Probably about fifteen minutes."

"Okay, then. I'll see you in about two hours."

Amused, he said, "It won't take you that long, but be careful and call me if you need me."

"Okay. Bye."

"See you in a bit."

Deja shifted the car in drive and proceeded to one of the resort roads. The road was free of snow, but looked slick, like a thin layer of ice was coating it. It probably was. She couldn't slide off the road doing five miles per hour, could she?

She kept on inching along. So far, so good. She even had enough confidence to dial Kris after she came to a sliding stop at the intersection of another resort road.

"Yo," he answered.

"I ought to come over there and pop you upside your bald head."

Kris chuckled. "Dare must've called you?"

"Yes, and now I'm on the way over there. I

told you not to call him…you….you…hardheaded little twit."

Kris laughed. "Why wouldn't I call him? He likes you."

"*Like* me? He doesn't *like* me."

Kris chuckled. "You poor little thing. Sariah was right. You do need to get out more."

Her mouth dropped open. "First of all, don't be worrying about what I'm doing. Mind yo' business."

"Dare is my business, and you *do* need to get out more if you can't tell when a guy is into you."

"Dare isn't *into* me. We're like…um…friends."

"No, you're…like…not," he said teasingly, imitating her voice. "Look…Dare is not as outgoing as me—"

"Thank goodness for that!" Deja said, then laughed.

"Hush, girl. As I was saying, Dare is the exact opposite of me, but when he's comfortable with someone, he'll open up to them. So, make him comfortable, *déjà vu*."

"Boy!" she yelled, gripping the steering tighter after veering off the pavement. After she got back on track, she said, "You almost made me run into the ditch. I told you to stop calling me that."

"Stop fronting like you don't like it. And make sure you ask Dare about the wedding. There have been some updates."

"What updates? Sariah didn't tell me anything has changed."

"I told you to ask Dare. It'll give you something to talk about. Bye."

He ended the call. Now, as she drove carefully, making her way to Dare's house following the GPS directions on her phone, she wondered exactly what changes Kris was referring to. She wanted to call Sariah, but she probably *would* end up in the ditch after a conversation with her, so she kept on driving. According to the navigation, she should arrive at Dare's house in twelve minutes. Only thing was, the GPS didn't account for snow and ice. She'd probably be there in about thirty or so.

CHAPTER 12

SHE ARRIVED THIRTY minutes later. She knew she was at the right house because his truck was parked in the driveway and the home looked big enough to house the five bedrooms he'd mentioned. It was a simple design – a white house with a large front porch and blue shutters around the windows. The grounds were covered in snow, of course, but he'd made sure the driveway was clear. When she stepped out of the car, she could hear the sound of salt crunching beneath her shoes. She opened the trunk and pulled out her suitcase, lowering it to the ground and extending the handle.

Dare stepped outside wearing a red sweater, jeans and boots. He saw the trunk open but didn't see Deja until he reached the car. She was leaning inside the trunk, reaching for something.

"Need some help?" Dare asked. "Any further and you'll be all the way in there."

She climbed out and stood straight up,

brushing off her jeans. "I'm good. I was trying to figure out which bag my socks were in, but I think I might've put them in the suitcase." She closed the trunk, then gave him a full sweep. She was convinced – red *must've* been his color because he looked gorgeous in it. It brought out those magnificent eyes of his.

She cleared her throat and said, "Okay…we're doing this." She grabbed the handle of the suitcase, but Dare said, "I got it."

"No worries. I can manage," she told him.

"Sure you can, but I don't want you to have to pull your suitcase through all of this salt." He pushed the extended handle down and picked up the suitcase by one of its handles and said, "I got it."

"You most certainly do," she told him. She could see those biceps putting in work.

As they walked toward the house, she said, "So, this is the place."

"Yes. This is it."

"It's huge."

"Yeah. I built it to contain every, single detail I wanted in a house. I'll be happy to show you around."

"Oh, I get the VIP treatment? Nice!"

He grinned. "Yes, you'll get the VIP treatment. It's not like we have anything else to do, Deja."

When they reached the stairs to the porch, Dare said, "Watch your step. I try to keep these stairs as clean as possible, but there could be some slick spots. I know how you like to slip and slide."

She giggled. "Yeah, that's the story of my Shenandoah Valley life."

She stomped off her boots and immediately after stepping inside, she slid off her boots, leaving them by the door.

Dare looked down at her feet and asked, "Where are your socks?"

"I think they're in the suitcase. I couldn't find them, so I put the boots on."

Dare chuckled. "I'll get you some socks."

"Oh, that's not necessary. My toes will thaw out after a while."

Dare looked down at her toes, paying particular interest to the way her toenails were painted – white polish with black polka dots.

She wiggled them, prompting him to look up at her with a smirk on his face.

"Looks like your toes got a case of the chickenpox."

"You don't like my pedicure?"

"It's nice…just different. I usually see women wearing a single color. You added a little something extra."

"I have to mix it up a bit."

"I can see that. I'll still get you some socks. Be right back, unless you want to come with me. You're more than welcome to."

"I think I'll wait here," she said with her arms crossed, looking around the place like she'd walked into the lobby of a fancy hotel.

"You can look around. Make yourself comfortable."

"Okay."

Dare jogged upstairs and Deja took in the scope of the place. The woodwork was impeccable. Everything was done with precision. The man surely was good with his hands to pull off this massive work of art. The house lacked nothing from what she could see. The wooden floors were warm to her bare feet since he had the fireplace blazing in the living room area. The smell of coffee lured her to the kitchen. That's where he must've been when she pulled up. She saw a coffee cup on the table with an opened laptop.

She looked over at the counter. There was plenty of coffee in the pot at the coffeemaker. Deciding to help herself, she went about searching the cabinets for a coffee mug. Two cabinets in and she still hadn't found what she was looking for.

"Hmm…where can I find a cup in this place?" she said evenly.

"Over here," he said, startling her.

She gasped. She hadn't heard him return. "Oh. Hey! Do you mind if steal some of your coffee?"

"Not at all. Help yourself to whatever you'd like. Don't ask me for anything."

She didn't want to go into the man's house and take over. And usually when people gave you

free rein in their home, they did it to be nice –
not because they meant it. Dare, being the
gentleman he was, surely was doing that – being
nice.

She chewed her lip and asked, "What happens
if I ask for something?"

"You'll get in trouble."

She smiled when she watched his provocative
smile amplify the handsome features on his face.
He was much more relaxed in his home
environment. She liked that.

He opened the cupboard and handed her a
cup.

"Thank you."

"You're welcome."

Deja poured herself some coffee and said,
"Oh, goodness. It smells delicious. What kind of
coffee is this?"

"It's local. You can't get this in Chapel Hill.
Kris always takes some back when he comes to
visit."

"I see." She added some half-and-half he'd left
on the counter and a spoonful of sugar. She took
a sip and closed her eyes. "Mmm…so good."

"Come sit down for a minute. You need to
relax after that harrowing drive."

"The drive wasn't all that bad."

"Really, because it took you almost an hour to
get here."

"I had to take my time."

"I know you had a line of cars behind you like,

what is this old lady doing on the road."

Deja laughed. "Oh, that's what we're doing now?"

"I'm just playing around with you. But for real though, have a seat."

"Where? At the table?"

"Wherever you feel comfortable."

She walked over to the table where he'd left his cup.

Dare followed her there, lowered himself to his knees and reached to touch her feet. He did it so quickly, she didn't have time to react, and that was intentional. He squeezed her feet into his palm. Deja's body jerked.

"Yeah, you need socks. Your feet feel like ice."

He slid on a pair of white socks on her feet, one by one.

The action brought a smile to her face. "Dare, I can put on my own socks."

"But these aren't your socks. They're my socks."

She fashioned a smile. "Still, I'm capable of putting them on."

"Not while you're drinking coffee, my dear," he said, standing.

"Well, thank you…got a girl feeling like Cinderella over here."

He smirked, stood up and took his coffee mug to the pot to get a refill. He was back just as quickly, sitting across from her. Looking at her. Taking in the fact she was here, in his home. He liked her here. It felt nice to share this space with someone again, even if she would be here for only one day.

She looked at him, caught his stare and shied away from it, taking another sip of coffee. She looked up again, thinking he wouldn't be staring so hard *this* time, but he was.

"What?" he asked.

"I can't believe you've rescued me again." She took a quick look at his long fingers wrapped around the coffee mug as he looked at her.

"It's not a problem, really, and while I have it on my mind, I wanted to apologize to you for yesterday. It was a mess. I left you there and it was tacky of me to do that…to engage in a conversation with my ex while we were together. You didn't need to see any of that and—"

"It's okay. It wasn't your fault. Um…I wasn't trying to listen, but I heard some of what she was saying. I had no idea the guy she cheated with was your best friend. I can imagine how humiliating that is for you, so no, you don't need to apologize to me for anything."

"I do," he said. "I was rude to leave like that. I shouldn't allow someone to bring me out of my character no matter what was said."

Deja nodded while listening intently.

He continued, "I had a chance to talk to Kris and my folks about it. They were over here last night…said it was a surprise dinner, but it felt more like an intervention."

"What kind of intervention?"

"One where they shake the life out of me and tell me how I need to move on with my life and stop letting what happened in the past ruin all the good that would come in the future."

"They're right."

"Yeah, they are."

"Is that what you feel you've been doing for the last six years?"

"I have, but it's time for me to get out of the past and start living." He sipped coffee. "As men, we tend to hold things inside—so much fear and—"

"Fear? You look like you can come out on the winning end of wrestling a bear. What *fear* do you have?"

He examined her briefly. For the first time, he felt this want, this desire to reveal what was on his heart. He said, "I appreciate the confidence boost, but I do have real fears, Deja. I fear being labeled a failure. Of being alone. I have a *real* fear that I'll never have the family I want. I'll never have love—a wife who loves and cherishes me like the vows say. I'll never have children to make this house a home—a house I built for them. I want all of those things, and even if I find a woman to share that with, I fear I'll end up running her away with all of my baggage."

"You won't," she said confidently.

"How do you know that?"

"Because you'll be extra careful with the

woman you select to give your heart to. We learn from experiences—good and bad ones—and you've learned a lot from yours, no matter how painful it was. You'll fall in love again. You're too good of a man not to. And the woman who catches your eye…she'll have a past of her own to share with you and, like you're talking to me now, you'll tell her all the things you've been through. If she truly cares for you, she'll listen and offer advice. She won't betray your trust or break your heart. So, yes, you'll be fine."

Deja looked up from the coffee mug, holding his gaze as he stared intently at her.

"Thanks for saying that."

"You're welcome."

"You sound like my mother."

Her eyes brightened when she asked, "She told you the same things?"

"Just about."

"Cool. You should listen to the women in your life."

"Yes, I should, and I will." He offered her a smile and she smiled back. "I would offer you breakfast, but I don't cook that well."

"What did you eat?"

"I usually sip coffee until lunch time, then run out and get something, but it doesn't look like there'll be no running out today. I was supposed to meet Kris at the store to try on my tux. We had to postpone."

"Well, I can whip up something real quick if

you have food."

"Yes, I have food, Deja."

"What? I didn't know. I just got here." She grinned. "Do you mind if I—?"

"Don't ask questions. Whatever you want to do, help yourself."

She stood up and walked to the fridge. Her eyes grew wide when she opened the door. "Good gawd! You have plenty of food! You must've stocked up before the storm."

"I sent Jolene shopping for me. She just buys stuff."

"Well, she certainly knocked it out of the park. You got green beans, potatoes, tomatoes…"

Dare chuckled. "Funny."

Deja took out a carton of eggs and a pack of bacon. After Dare showed her where to find the frying pans, cooking oil and utensils, she whipped up a fast breakfast. There was a loaf of wheat bread on the counter, so she toasted two pieces to go along with the food.

She set a plate on the table for Dare, then sat across from him.

"You moved right in, huh?"

"Yeah. They say once you feed a girl, it's hard to get her to leave."

"I'm sure whoever *they* are were referring to men when they made that statement."

He picked up a fork, tasted the eggs and said, "Mmm, the eggs are good."

"Why, thank you. I do what I can."

155

He smirked. "You didn't eat all those donuts last night, did you?"

"I was tempted, but no, they're in the backseat of my car. I wrapped the box in a sweater like a child and put the seatbelt around it."

"Please tell me you didn't buckle up some donuts."

"I would be lying if I told you that," she said, laughing until tears came to her eyes. "Gotta make sure my babies make it back to Chapel Hill safely." She looked over at him and watched the smile on his face slowly fall away as he stared back at her. She didn't know why he was staring so hard, but she'd watched him do it several times. A knot formed in her stomach. That's how sharply his bright eyes had honed in on her.

She took a bite of toast and could still feel his eyes on her. What was he staring at? *Why* was he staring? To get his eyes off of her, she said, "Kris told me you had an update about the wedding."

"I told him I would be his best man. I don't know if that's what he was referring to specifically."

"I thought you were already his best man."

"I wasn't. I didn't think I wanted to be after my failed marriage and he didn't ask me to be his best man, so I didn't mention it and neither did he. Yesterday, he made it clear."

"Do you know what that means?" She watched him sip coffee, paying particular interest to the groomed hair above his top lip.

"What does that mean?"

"It means you'll be escorting me down the aisle, which also means I need to find a pair of tall heels so we don't look weird walking together."

"You don't need heels."

"I do. Have you seen how tall you are?"

He broke into a grin. "I am tall, but you look good standing beside me without heels."

Deja smiled beneath the heat of yet another gaze he offered.

When Dare could stop staring at her, and that was becoming harder and harder to do, he finished eating the rest of his eggs then said, "So, tell me about you. What are your life plans?"

Deja shrugged. "I just want to be happy. I don't have a list or anything."

"I mean, what about marriage? Or, dare I say, a child you can buckle into the back seat instead of a bag of donuts."

"Hey, leave my donuts out of this," she said, laughing. "But, yes, I want children, a family—all of that."

"Why aren't you pursuing that?"

"Who says I haven't been?"

"I'm saying that, and I could be wrong, but I've been sitting here looking at you and you're giving off these vibes like you're fine with your life the way it is."

"I am, to a degree. I think there's some truth to living life and letting love find you. That's what I'm waiting for. I don't want anything that feels fake or rushed."

Dare beamed at her response. She was unbelievable and he was having an unbelievably amazing time with her being here having a conversation with him. He hated it to come to an end, but they still had the rest of the day.

He said, "Since we're stuck indoors, I guess we'll have to make the most of it. Do you play cards?"

"Nope."

"No? I thought for sure you'd say yes."

"I've never been into cards," Deja told him. "I play solitaire on my phone now and then. If you want to play a game, I suggest something like hide-n-seek."

"You're not joking, are you?"

"Nope. There're a lot of hiding spots in this house. That's the first thing that came to mind when I walked up in here."

"O-kay. Well, I guess we're playing hide-n-seek tonight."

"Yeah. Let's do that. It'll do you some good."

"How so?"

"Other than the time you took me snow tubing, you're always so…what's the word I'm looking for…"

"Boring?"

"No, not boring. You're mellow…nothing wrong with that, but it doesn't hurt to find your inner child now and then and be free."

"You think so?"

"Mmm-hmm," she said, then sipped coffee. "Remember when we were kids and didn't have a care in the world and had a zest for life? I think we should live that way as adults. Life is meant to be lived and enjoyed. Since being here in the valley, I got to thinking about how much I wasn't enjoying mine back home. It's all about *work, work, work* with me, but I need some playtime, too. So do you, Dare Stokes."

A slow smile spread across Dare's face. "I'll keep that in mind."

CHAPTER 13

SHE COULD GET used to this…

Hours ago, Dare had given her a tour of the place and afterward, she returned to the sunroom where she sat with her laptop and did a little work for a new client. However, concentration proved difficult when she could look through the wall of windows that surrounded her and see the snow falling. The white flakes dwindled down slowly, drifting to join the inches that had already accumulated over the past week. The snowcapped trees looked picturesque and divinely serene. Deja wasn't a fan of snow, but the view — it was simply amazing.

"Beautiful, isn't it?"

Deja looked up to see Dare standing in the doorway. Earlier in the day, he had on a red sweater and jeans. He must've gotten hot because he switched out his sweater for a short-sleeved V-neck shirt. With his arms crossed, she could see the definition of his biceps — and boy were they impressive. And then those jeans...they rode his hips like a well-trained cowboy on a mechanical bull. She was certain his thighs were as toned and taut as his arms, but she had to use her imagination for that. He wasn't wearing shoes or socks. He was comfortable in his home. She liked that.

"Deja?"

"Huh?"

"Did you hear me?"

"Um...no. I was so busy thinking about the um...this new...um...client." *More like busy checking you out.* "What did you say?"

"I saw you staring out the window. I asked if you like the view."

Yes, she loved the view – all six-feet-three inches of the view. She understood why he took off his sweater. He was *hott* with two T's. Dare had it going on and it wasn't just his incredibly good looks. He was an overall good, wholesome man.

Deja cleared her throat and said, "Yes. It's so nice to be inside a warm, cozy home watching the snow shower outside. Thanks again for letting me stay here."

"You're welcome. Now stop thanking me for that. It's cool."

"Okay," she said, hands up. "So, what have you been up to? Did you take a nap, or—I'm sorry...I shouldn't be asking you what you were doing like it's any of my business."

Dare sauntered over to her and sat on the sofa. He said, "I told you I had to get some work done."

"Yeah, that was like four hours ago. You've been held up in your office for four hours straight?"

"Yes."

"Must've been a lot of work."

"It was. It's a challenge looking for the right materials for these houses. I'm looking for a specific kind of pebble for a shower floor I'm designing in one of the houses. For another house, I need subway tiles. And the flooring—I can't tell you how difficult it is to find cherry wood."

"Hmm…" she said.

"What?"

"Nothing," she said, shoving her question to the side.

"Tell me. You look like you have a question."

"I was wondering about the pebbles for the shower. I've never seen that before."

"Yeah, it's different, but pebbles are not slippery like most shower floors. I think it's the safer option, so much so I've been contemplating doing my showers like that."

"That's pretty cool. I like how you get to design these houses and you know how to carry out the design. You did a phenomenal job on this place."

Deja stretched and yawned.

Dare said, "Tired?"

"I shouldn't be. I took a nap earlier."

"I know. I came in here to check on you and saw you laid out. One leg was up here on the backrest and the other was hanging off the couch."

"Oh no…how embarrassing," she said, red-cheeked.

"I took a selfie with you and posted it on Insta."

She gasped. "You did not!"

Laughing, he said, "No, I didn't." He rubbed his hands together and said, "I did, however, spread a blanket on you."

"Aw…you're too kind. Thank you, Dare. This—all of this—is just so much. I'll repay you one day."

"There's nothing to repay me for, Deja."

"It is. I mean, you've done a lot for me over the past week."

And you've done a lot for me, too. That's what Dare wanted to say. She'd brought out a spark in him that had been missing for years, and her presence in his home produced more warmth than the blazing fireplace. And he enjoyed how she took an interest in his work.

"What's on the agenda now that you've come up for air?"

Dare glanced at his watch. "It's getting close to dinnertime."

"I could cook something," Deja offered.

Her eyes were bright and eager, Dare noticed, but he didn't bring her here to be his cook. He said, "You already cooked breakfast—"

"That took all of ten minutes. I can whip up something fast for dinner. It's not like we can order pizza or something. The delivery drivers can't navigate this snow, especially now that night's falling. The roads will get worse."

"You're right."

"I'll go see what you have in the refrigerator and pantry, then determine what I can prepare— that's if I can find my way back to the kitchen."

She stood up.

"This house is not big enough for you to get lost."

"Oh, yes, it is! I've already been scoping out some bomb spots for me to hide when we play hide-n-seek tonight."

Dare stood up and followed her to the kitchen, saying, "Yes, but you have to remember, it's my house. I know when something is out of order. I'm sure I'll find you very easily. You, on the other hand, will *never* find me."

"Never say never." Stepping into the kitchen, she went straight to the refrigerator and upon opening the freezer door, she saw a pack of ground beef. She checked the pantry for spaghetti noodles and sauce, then turned to him and said, "I can cook some spaghetti. What do you think?"

"That's fine with me. I haven't had spaghetti in a while."

She used the defrost function on the microwave to thaw out the meat, then asked, "Here's a question. If you don't cook, why do you have all of this food?"

"I never said I didn't cook. I said I don't cook well."

She smiled. "Oh. Gotcha."

"I be in this kitchen making a mess sometimes. And I eat whatever I cook no matter how bad it turns out."

"Hey, at least you're not letting anything go to waste."

"Exactly. That's how I look at it."

"Well, it'll take me about an hour to prepare this, so if you want to go back to your office and do some work—"

"I'd much rather watch you cook. I'm going to bring my laptop in here."

"Okay," she said. He exited the kitchen and she shook her head. *I'd rather watch you cook*, he'd said. Little did he know she'd rather watch *him* work with his handsome self. Heather had to be out of her mind to walk away from a hardworking, handsome man like Dare. He was a man who knew how to work with his hands, commit to a woman and come home every day instead of running the streets. Was that Heather's definition of boring?

* * *

165

"DINNER WAS DELICIOUS," Dare said. "I don't think I've ever had baked spaghetti."

"No?"

"No. I've always had it with plain noodles and a scoop of sauce on top."

"Yeah, I call that the fancy way. I like it that way, too, but baking ensures you get the cheese and everything up in there real good."

"I agree. It was very good. Thank you for cooking."

"You're welcome."

Dare leaned back in his chair, full and satisfied.

Deja said, "I'm going to go up and take a shower so, after I kick your butt at hide-n-seek, I can go straight to bed."

"Oh, is that right?"

"Yep. I'll be back down shortly."

"Take your time."

Deja went upstairs, saw a missed call from Sariah and ignored it. She didn't want to hear anything else from her sister about the wedding. That could wait until she returned home.

She dug out a pajama set from her suitcase. Thank goodness she'd washed all of her clothes during her last night's stay at the condo. At least she didn't have to bug Dare about using his washer and dryer.

She showered quickly, put on some lotion, then returned downstairs so they could get the game started. But there was a problem. Dare was nowhere to be found. She figured she'd clean up in the kitchen until he returned, but upon entering the kitchen, she found it already tidied up. He'd washed the dishes and put the rest of the spaghetti in the fridge.

"Hmm," she said. *He must've called it a night…*

She looked at the table where they'd been sitting for dinner and saw a piece of yellow paper that looked out of place. She walked over, picked it up and saw a note that said:

Find me.

"You sneaky little…"

A smile instantly came to her face when she realized he'd started the game early. He was hiding, waiting for her to find him.

"Oh, that's so not fair, Dare!"

Grinning, she said in a monotone, "I have no idea where to look." Where *was* the first place to start looking in this big house? She decided to begin downstairs first then work her way up if she had to. She checked the laundry room. She peeked into the pantry. She checked under the tables in the two downstairs bathrooms. She looked in the sunroom, the living room and the coat closet. She checked the master suite – the only bedroom downstairs.

He was nowhere to be found.

"Okay, so you must be upstairs somewhere?" she reasoned, standing at the base of the stairs, leery about going up.

A daunting task lay ahead of her. Not only were there four bedrooms upstairs – there were also their accompanying closets, the man cave, another living room and two bathrooms.

She took the stairs slowly and when she got to the top, she said, "I know you're up here somewhere, Dare?"

She cautiously pushed the door of the first bedroom – the room where she would be sleeping. She checked under the bed. She checked in the closet. He wasn't there.

In the second bedroom, she did the same. She checked the bedroom across the hallway and the bathroom adjacent to it. She looked inside the remaining two bedrooms and the living room. The only room left upstairs to check was the man cave.

Deja took a deep breath before opening the door. Dare had shown her around this morning, so she knew about the man cave and the bar. He could've hidden behind the bar, or maybe behind the leather sofa. Yeah, that's where he was – behind the sofa. From where she was standing, it looked like it was moved up away from the wall a little, so he had to be behind there, right?

She tipped closer, bent down and said, "Aha! Gotcha!"

But she didn't *have* him. He wasn't behind the sofa and he wasn't behind the bar either. Defeated, she turned around and headed out of the room. She returned to the top of the stairs and yelled, "Okay, I give up!"

"This is your game. You're not allowed to give up."

A clue!

His voice had come from downstairs, so at least now she knew where to narrow her search.

She descended the stairs, hoping he'd slip up and say something else, but all was quiet when her feet landed off the last step and onto the floor. She closed her eyes and tried to concentrate on where his voice might've come from. If she had to use her best educated guess, it sounded like it had come from the living room.

But she had checked the living room already. She went there and started over again, searching for anything that looked like he could hide behind. With that tall, lengthy body of his, there wasn't much he could hide behind.

"OMG...it shouldn't take twenty minutes for me to find you," Deja said quietly.

"No, it shouldn't," Dare responded.

Deja nearly jumped out of her skin when she turned around and watched him come from behind the drapes. With her hand on her heart, she said, "You scared the daylights out of me!"

Dare folded over, laughing. "You're right. This is fun."

She was still trying to control her fast-beating heart and catch her breath while she was busy laughing it up.

"Alright, it's your turn to hide," he told her.

"Nah, I'm good."

Still laughing himself breathless, he said, "I thought you said…you…you needed to find your inner child."

"Oh, I found my inner child—I found a whole toddler when I peed on myself after you jumped out from behind those curtains."

"It wasn't that bad, was it?"

"It was. I gotta get some water."

He trailed her to the kitchen. She drank and said, "I just knew you were in your man cave, but how wrong was I?"

"Yeah, you weren't even close."

"That's because you have the advantage since this is your house. Plus, you cheated."

He snickered. "How did I cheat?"

"Because…you hid after I went up to shower."

"I beat you at your own game."

"You sure did. I'm not even gon' hide because you'll find me in like three seconds."

He smiled. Of course, I would. I know this house like the back of my hand. "I was thinking you should probably hit the sack. You have a long drive ahead of you."

"Ugh. I know, and I'm not looking forward to it."

He wasn't looking forward to her leaving either. He'd be constantly worried about her being alone on the road, even if the highways were clear.

She yawned.

"Okay, Deja. Get to bed. I'll see you in the morning."

"Yeah," she said solemnly. She wasn't ready to leave either, but she knew she couldn't stay.

She stepped closer to him and closed her arms around his torso, feeling his warmth soothe her. A girl could get used to this, but Dare's heart was unavailable and she was very well aware of that. "Goodnight, Dare."

"Goodnight, Deja," he said, gently stroking her back.

She pulled back and headed upstairs.

He stood there, watching her walk away, wondering how his life would return to normal after she was gone.

* * *

A HIGH-PITCHED whistling noise awakened Deja in the middle of the night. She sat up in bed. The dark room added to her angst. She flicked on the bedside lamp. Why did creepy nighttime noises seem to go away as soon as a light came on? Now, she didn't hear a thing. All was well, but after lying down again, she couldn't get back to sleep.

Annoyed, she sat up again, and this time traveled downstairs to the kitchen to get some water. She was careful to be quiet so as not to disturb Dare since his bedroom was downstairs. After she took a few sips of water, she walked to the sunroom where she'd napped earlier in the day. The room was dark, but the outside lights were shining bright enough to where it provided enough light so she could see her way around. She walked over to the window and stared at the snow again. The lights struck it in a way that showcased its beauty. Tomorrow, she'd be on her way home. She would miss this place. The valley. The snow. *Him.*

"Can't sleep?"

Deja turned around to see Dare walking into the room. He didn't have on a shirt – only a pair of sweatpants.

She swallowed hard. She knew he had muscles, but this was taking it to a whole new level! She wasn't expecting such a broad chest amplified by chiseled pectorals, well-defined bulky shoulders, and beefy arms that looked like they could carry anything. And she wasn't about to dwell on those sweatpants. The way they hung on his hips and...

"Deja?"

"Oh, um, I—I—"

Jeez. What did he ask me again? Oh!

"No, I couldn't sleep," Deja responded. "I kept hearing this strange whistling noise. I came down here to get some water, and the view lured me back into this room."

Dare took position next to her beside the windows. "The noise is caused by the wind. Just looking out the window, it looks calm, peaceful and serene out there. It's very deceiving. The wind is whipping out there."

"Oh. I see."

"If you'd like, you can sleep in here. The sofa converts to a bed."

"Oh, now you tell me."

He chuckled. "I couldn't tell you earlier. You were already passed out."

Dare walked to the sofa, reached for the bar beneath it and pulled it open, converting the sofa to a bed. "There. I use this a lot when I don't want to sleep in my bedroom."

"You'd go for the sofa bed over that huge bed in your bedroom?"

"Yeah. I try not to think about certain things when I'm in my bedroom, but sometimes, whether I want to or not, my mind goes there."

"Is that why you're up tonight?"

"Yep. Hey, I'll go grab you some pillows and covers."

Deja paced the area beside the sofa bed with her arms crossed and after a few minutes of doing so, Dare was back with a handful of pillows and covers. He spread a sheet over the mattress first, then tossed the pillows there. Afterward, he gestured for her to lie down and when she did, he spread a comforter over her.

"I hope you sleep better in here."

"I'm sure I will. What time is it?"

"It's a little after two."

"Okay."

"Alright. Goodnight again, Deja."

Deja didn't say anything, so Dare turned to leave the room. She didn't want him to leave. But could she ask him to stay? She contemplated doing so, chewing her lip to get up the nerve. Before he reached the door, she blurted out, "Can you stay with me?"

Dare stopped, turned around and looked at her. He didn't say anything for a moment – just stood there. Then he said, "Okay," and walked back over to the sofa bed. He didn't know how close she wanted him – *close*, close or somewhere in the room. He got his answer when she moved over, giving him a spot on the bed. He sat down first, then slowly laid down next to her. Reluctantly. Cautiously.

With eyes full of sleep, she looked at him. She could feel his warmth greeting her and they weren't even touching. And his delectable smell – she couldn't quite figure out the scent, but it was a pleasurable experience.

Her eyes fluttered as she pulled in a deep breath of his scent. His aura. Why was it so calming for her? She was ready to fall asleep but forced her eyes to stay open long enough to look at him once more. He was staring straight up at the ceiling.

"Dare?"

Dare turned to look at her. The color of his eyes took up residence in her short and long-term memory. She'd never seen a man with such beautiful eyes – with so much beautiful *everything* –

and yet he was so grounded and humble. That to her was more desirable than his looks.

She said, "I hope this isn't weird for you?"

"It's not."

"I kind of get the sense that it is, and trust me, it's weird for me, too, so when I fall asleep, which won't be long, you can go back to your room, okay?"

"So, you're just gon' use me and throw me away?"

Deja giggled softly. "It sounds so bad when you put it like that, but you're the one who said I needed sleep since I have a long drive ahead of me tomorrow."

"You do."

"Yes." She yawned. "I certainly do."

Dare listened as soft hums began drifting her away. She wouldn't have any problems sleeping in here. Was it the comfortability of the room, or the fact that he was here with her? Probably a little of both.

"Dare." She'd called his name with her eyes closed.

"Yes?" he asked, looking at her sweet, gorgeous face, admiring the delicate features of her as he waited for her to say something. Her lips were super soft. He didn't have to touch them to know that.

"Do you think the roads will be clear in the morning?"

"They should be clear enough for you to make

it home safely."

Even though I wouldn't mind if you stayed another day or two.

"Okay." Deja dozed off, then when she felt Dare move, she opened her eyes again and said, "You can go back to your room now. Mmm…I'm almost out."

"What if I don't want to go back to my room?"

Deja's eyes were still closed. He watched a smile come to her face and moved closer to her, instinctively pulling her close to him. As if she'd done it a thousand times before, Deja tucked her head beneath his chin and placed the palm of her right hand against his pectoral.

Dare's breath caught in his throat. He hadn't been this close to a woman since Heather. The feeling of Deja in his arms had him thinking about all kinds of things – like how much he missed sharing his life with someone. The conversations. The companionship. The intimacy. The love.

His mother was right. The house was nice. The job was rewarding. But nothing could compare to the love, care and attention of a woman. The *right* woman. And he may have found her – the beautiful woman tucked safely in his arms.

CHAPTER 14

DEJA WAS ROLLING down the highway doing seventy miles per hour when she looked briefly at her ringing phone. Dare was calling. She had expected a call from him, especially since she had carefully pried his arms from around her and snuck out of the house this morning without so much as a goodbye.

She answered, "Hello."

"Good morning, Deja."

"Good morning, Dare."

"Please tell me you're not on your way home."

"I am."

"Why did you leave so soon, and without saying goodbye?"

"I left you a note. I figured it would be less awkward that way."

"I like awkward, and I like you. I wanted to say a proper goodbye. Now, I can't do that. It's not like I can embrace this piece of paper."

A long pause filled the line. Dare asked, "What time did you leave?"

"Six."

"Wow. It's nine o'clock now. You're almost home."

"Yeah, I got another hour and some change to go."

"I wish you would've woken me up."

"I know. I'm sorry. But, hey, I'll be back in two weeks with the family. And, I'll see you at rehearsal."

"When is rehearsal? Kris hasn't updated me on all of that yet."

"It's the day before the wedding."

"Okay. Two whole weeks away, huh?"

"Yeah."

"And who am I supposed to play hide-n-seek with while you're gone?"

She grinned. "Stop talking like that. You're making me feel guilty."

"I'm teasing you. Listen, pay attention to the road, drive safely, watch out for the crazy people and call me when you make it home."

"Okay, I will."

"I'll talk to you later, Deja."

"Okay. Bye."

"Bye."

She placed the phone in the passenger seat and smiled from ear to ear.

What a man!

But he was a man with issues. Realistically, who wouldn't have issues if their spouse left and ran off with the best friend? And years later, those actions still held him hostage. He'd be the perfect match for her if he wasn't stuck. Still, she couldn't fault him for being that way.

People didn't fully understand what they did to the innocent person when they cheated, especially when that person was a man. Most times, society singled out men as cheaters, but what about when they're *not* cheaters? What happens to the faithful, hardworking men who committed themselves to the wrong woman? That's what Dare had done, and because of what had happened to him, he was binding himself to a life of loneliness, fearing the same thing could happen to him again.

Paying attention to the GPS on her phone, Deja took the next exit. She'd never been infatuated with anyone. There were no secret crushes from her past, or *potentials* even though her sister always had some guy she thought would be the perfect fit for her, but something about Dare spoke to her soul and made her want to get to know him beyond the surface – way beyond the *hi* and *bye*. Beyond spending one night with him and a few dinners. She wanted to know his pain. She wanted to help him navigate through it so that, after his rehabilitation, he'd open his eyes and see her as a viable candidate – a woman who wouldn't crush his soul but nourish it.

* * *

AS SOON AS she arrived home, Deja called

Dare as he had requested.

He said, "I bet it feels good to be home."

"It does," she told him, but it was bittersweet. She missed him already. If she lived in Harrisonburg, they could hang out more and he'd get to learn to trust her and who knows – they could start their own love story instead of being a part of their siblings' fairytales. But his heart wasn't ready for anything like that, she knew.

"I'm glad you arrived safely."

"Thanks."

"I trust your donuts arrived unscathed."

She laughed. "Some of them didn't make it. I had myself a snack break."

"I bet." He grinned.

"I was a little sad when I got here."

"Why?"

Because you weren't here.

"Um…there was no snow. It's sixty degrees here today. I got out of my car and walked to the door without doing the Cha-Cha slide."

He chuckled. "I thought you'd like that."

"I did. I just…I had so much fun in Shenandoah Valley. I'm looking forward to coming back."

"Come back anytime. Don't be a stranger, Deja," he said, "And I mean that."

Deja could hear the resolve in his voice when he made the statement.

"I won't."

"I mean it. And if I ever cross your mind,

please don't hesitate to call."

"Same to you."

"Really?" he asked.

"Yes."

"In that case, I'll be calling you regularly," he told her.

Warmth crawled over her skin. "Okay, Dare. Thanks again for everything. I owe you big time."

"You owe me nothing, sweetheart. Get some rest, and I'll talk to you later."

"Okay. Bye."

She hung up the phone and pushed out a sigh, looking around at her apartment. Why did it feel so lonely all of a sudden? This was her haven, the place where she felt free to explore and express herself. The place where she worked, lived and relaxed. Today, however, she wasn't relaxing. She was battling her emotions. She was physically here in her Chapel Hill apartment, but she'd left her mind and possibly her heart in Shenandoah Valley with a handsome gentleman named Dare.

CHAPTER 15

A Week Later

DARE SAT IN his work truck, cranked up the heat and waited for Dillon to walk over so they could go grab some lunch. The houses – the two they were currently concentrating their efforts on this month – were coming along nicely. He looked around at the houses they'd finished last year, the ones closest to the highway, and thought about how this land used to be nothing but trees. They'd transformed it into a middle-class neighborhood where families would start their lives. It brought him great satisfaction knowing that.

He drove to Arby's and after they ordered, they sat in the restaurant to eat for a change. Usually, Dare would grab some food and head back out to the work site – especially on a Monday. Today, he wanted to slow down and take time to enjoy lunch.

Dillon unwrapped his sandwich and started talking about the houses – more specifically, where they were on the completion of the entire project. Normally, Dare would be all for it, only today, he didn't want to discuss houses. He wanted to talk about something different. Some*one* different.

After taking a bite of his roast beef sandwich, he cut into Dillon's conversation and said, "It's amazing how much you can miss someone."

Dillon looked at him and shook his head.

Dare took a sip of tea and continued. He said, "Just when I thought those feelings were long gone, they come back to the surface. I guess they always come back for the *right* person."

Dillon couldn't believe what he was hearing. Dare had it bad for his ex and he couldn't understand why. The whole thing was frustrating. He said, "Heather hurt you to your core. How can you *possibly* still have feelings for her after all this time?"

"Dillon—"

"No, hear me out. Dare, you're my friend and my boss, but I'm just gon' to say it. It's time for you to snap out of it and move on with your life, or I'ma haul off and knock some sense into you, man."

Dare smirked and leaned back a little. "You're funny."

"I'm not playing with you, bro. You deserve better. There're so many women out there. Good women. Women who wouldn't do what Heather did to you. Why are you so hung up on her?"

"I'm not. I wasn't talking about Heather just now."

"Then I must've missed something."

"Let me fill you in. Remember the woman who was broke down beside the road? The one I helped?"

"Yeah."

"Turns out, she's the sister of my brother's fiancée. I've been hanging out with her."

"That's good, man."

"Yeah, I thought so, too. She went back home a week ago. She's who I was referring to."

"What's her name?"

"Deja," Dare responded, then took another bite.

"Deja…I like her already."

Dare nodded. "She's a breath of fresh air. I think I needed that."

"What do you like about her?" Dillon questioned.

Dare smiled and said, "Everything. Do you know what's weird about it?"

"What's that?"

"The moment I picked her up from beside the road, I knew there was something about her. I could sense it. I never thought I'd get to the point where I would meet a woman who would ignite something inside of me. I thought that part died with my failed marriage, but it didn't die. It just took the right person to resurrect it, which got me to thinking…what if those six long, painful years after my divorce were preparing me for this—for a new beginning. For her. For Deja."

"Then I say you served your time. Now, it's time to live. When will you see her again?"

"In a few weeks."

"Nice."

"I'm seriously contemplating making a surprise visit to see her this weekend."

"So, you can't wait until the wedding to see her."

"No. I want to see her now."

"That's a good sign. Real good, Dare. She must've made some impression on you, so, go."

"You really think I should?"

"Yeah, man. This is the first time I've seen a real smile on your face in six years. Go."

"Ah'ight. I think I will."

CHAPTER 16

"UGH, THIS BLOWS!" Deja said as she scheduled social media posts for her client's cleaning business. The client had requested she include funny quotes about cleaning, but she couldn't come up with any. Normally, that wasn't a problem for her, but since returning home from Shenandoah Valley, she hadn't been able to concentrate as much as she would've liked. She was too busy thinking about Dare, even during the times after she supposedly had given herself a talking to. It had been three full days since she last saw him. She still had images of him embedded into her permanent memory – like when he'd walked into the café, the way he bit into a donut and the smile on his face when they went snow tubing – not to mention his most gorgeous resting face when she had to sneak out of bed to go home.

When she'd opened her eyes Monday morning, it was like a dream had come true. She imagined she was the one in love, getting married and waking up to a husband – a man who would shower her with love and protect her. Give her pretty, little yellow babies and live happily ever after.

Dang.

If only he were hers.

She'd show him how a woman treats a real man. She'd cook dinners for him. They'd play hide-n-seek and when the kids came along and were old enough, they'd run all through the house playing laser tag and being one big happy family. Now that she'd had a taste of what it was like to spend time with a man, she wanted more of it, but not with any man. She wanted Dare Stokes.

She sighed, rubbed her temples and glanced at the clock on the bottom right corner of her computer. The time was a little after eleven. She was supposed to meet Sariah for lunch at noon to go over some last-minute wedding details. She wondered if she could meet her any earlier. Only one way to find out.

She dialed her sister's number.

Sariah answered, "Whazzzzup! How is my favorite sister doing on this lovely Thursday morning?"

At least somebody's in a good mood, Deja thought.

She asked, "Have you been drinking this morning or something?"

"Nope…just high off love, sis."

Deja smiled. She loved that her sister was in

love, although she couldn't stand the little *rodent* she was in love with, but still – she was happy and that's all that mattered. It must've been a good feeling.

Sariah continued, "And I closed on a house, which means, I'm fenna get paid!"

"Congratulations, Sariah."

"Thank you!"

"That also means you got lunch covered today, right?"

"Yep. Can you meet me right now? I'm not doing *anything* for the rest of the day. I'm in celebration mode all day!"

"Yeah, I can leave now," Deja said. It's not like she was doing anything either. "Where are we going?"

"Let's go to Cosmic. It's taco Tuesday, and I'm craving a burrito."

"That sounds good," Deja said, standing. Stretching. She closed her laptop, then walked over to the coat rack to grab a sweater.

* * *

WHEN DEJA ARRIVED at the restaurant Sariah waved her over, but the smile fell from Deja's face when she saw Kris sitting next to her. What was Kris doing here? This was supposed to be a *sister* lunch date, and he had to go ruining it.

Deja reluctantly walked over to the table, sat opposite of them and said, "You didn't tell me you asked clown-face to come, Sariah."

Kris snickered. "It's good to see you too, Deja."

Deja rolled her eyes. "Now, I don't have an appetite."

"No worries," Kris said. "I'll eat a burrito for you since you wanna be all stubborn."

"Ugh…" Deja crossed her arms. "Make it stop talking to me, Sariah."

Sariah was too busy staring at the menu to pay them any attention. Besides, she'd grown accustomed to their disdain for each other. It was as normal as breathing now.

Deja uncrossed her arms to glance at the menu. She asked, "Which burrito are you getting, Sariah?"

"The steak burrito with extra rice."

"I'll probably get the same," Deja said. "They have good rice here."

"I think I'll spring for the fajita," Kris said.

Deja glared. "Are you sure? It might pop one of your abdominal muscles out of the socket."

Kris laughed, then smiled at her. "Deja, stop pretending you don't like me."

"I'm not pretending."

He shook his head. "Well, you'll learn to like me. We're going to be seeing a lot more of each other. A *lot* more."

"Ugh…Kris, stick a pin in it already," Sariah said.

"Babe, it's your sister who's starting with me,"

he said, looking at Sariah like he could devour her. "You know I'm all about you." He leaned over and kissed her on the cheek, then grazed her neck with his teeth. Sariah laughed playfully and tried to jerk away from him, but he held her so she couldn't move.

"Kris…" she said, blushing as she looked at him and his attention immediately went to her lips. And he didn't hold anything back. He kissed her as if they were in the privacy of their own home, or in a car – anywhere else other than a packed restaurant, sitting in front of her single sister who didn't have a man or any prospects of one.

The waitress walked up and said, "Hi, guys. Are you all ready to order?"

Deja glanced up at Kris and Sariah still kissing and replied to the waitress, "I'm ready. If you bring me a butter knife, I can try to pry those two apart."

The waitress laughed. "They must be newlyweds, huh?"

"Almost. The wedding is a little over a week away."

"I knew it had to be something like that. If they'd been together for like five years, she'd be sitting where you're sitting right now."

Deja chuckled. "Is that how it works?"

"Chile, yes. Half the time, I be finding excuses to get away from my husband. Don't get me wrong, I love my man, but a sister needs some space."

"I hear ya."

"What can I get for you?"

"Me and my sister will have the steak burrito, both with an extra side of rice. That *thing* that's kissing her wants the steak fajita, and bring some extra tortillas because he's going to finish the entire thing."

"Sure thing. I'll bring that right out. Waters for everybody?"

"For now, yes. Thank you."

"Yep, no problem!"

Deja waited until the waitress walked away and said, "Um, hello. I didn't come to lunch to watch y'all make out."

Kris finally pulled away from Sariah and said, "Mmm...that was all the food I needed."

"Okay, good!" Deja said. "Bye! Run your tail on back to work then."

Kris smiled at her.

Deja narrowed her eyes. Why was he being all smiley with her today?

She jumped slightly when she felt a hand bear down on her shoulder. She turned around – her eyes grew big when they caught sight of the man she couldn't get off of her mind and the reason she couldn't focus at work – Dare Stokes. She leaped up from her seat and threw her arms around him, squeezing him – holding him as close and as tight to her as she could. She ended the hug to look at him. She said, "Are you—are you really here?"

He smiled. "Yes, I'm here, Deja."

"What are you doing here?" she asked, her heart thumping in her chest while surprise brightened her eyes.

"I wanted to talk to you."

"You can talk to me on the phone."

He beamed, looking down into her eyes. He said, "I know, Deja, but there's nothing like talking to you in person so I can see this pretty face of yours." He ran the back of his index finger along her cheek. Then he held her hand and looked at Kris and Sariah.

He said, "What's up, Kris?"

"You made it."

You made it. Now Deja knew why Kris had been smiling. He knew about this all along.

"I did," Dare replied. "And you must be Sariah."

"That's me," Sariah said.

"It's nice to meet you, Sariah."

"You as well, Dare," Sariah said. "Kris didn't tell me I would get to meet his brother today."

"That's because I didn't want Deja to find out I was coming." He looked at her lovingly and said, "I wanted to surprise her."

"It worked," Deja said.

"If you two would excuse me, I need to borrow Deja for a moment," Dare said.

"Please...take all the time you need," Kris said, but Deja was too off her game to hit him with a comeback.

Dare tightened the grip on her hand as they walked through the restaurant and out the door.

Deja asked, "Where are we going?"

"We can sit in my truck for a moment. I need to talk to you."

"Is everything all right, Dare?"

"Everything's fine. It's actually better than fine now that I'm here."

Dare opened the passenger side door for her. She stepped up and sat comfortably in the familiar seat. He walked around, hopped in the driver's seat, looked at her and said, "Hi."

She smiled. "Hi."

For a moment, they stared at each other, neither not saying a word or blinking.

She said, "Are you talking right now because I don't see your lips moving. I want to make sure you're not saying anything and I'm not hearing you because I'm so busy staring into your eyes. I'm sort of shocked that you're here and—"

"Deja."

"Yes?"

"I wasn't talking. I was just looking at you."

"Oh."

"But I do have something to say, so please bear with me as I try to get the words out."

"Okay," Deja said nervously since she didn't know what this was about. She didn't expect he'd show up here. Why was he here?

"For six years, I've been fighting my way

through life, secretly battling my feelings without telling a single soul what I was going through. For six years, I've been living in the dark, occupying myself with work to be able to make it from day to day because of what someone else did to me. For six years, I've…"

Dare paused and pulled in a much-needed breath – one that would help him bite back the pain he'd suffered. When he was able to speak again with a clear voice, he said, "For six years, I've suffered greatly. I told myself this was all there was for me now. Misery. Working. Going home alone. Watching TV alone. Doing *everything* alone. It's what I deserved for not being the man my ex needed me to be? Everything that had happened to me, I brought it upon myself. I took the blame for someone else's actions and buried myself with those sins as if they were my own. I'd given up—that is until I met this woman beside the road who, for the first time in a long time, made a smile come to my face. You do that constantly, so much so that when you left, Deja, I found myself smiling at the memories of you."

"Okay, stop talking," Deja said, fanning her eyes. "You're going to make me cry."

"I don't want to make you cry, but I need to say this."

Deja pinched tears from her eyes and said, "Okay."

"You don't know how much joy you've brought into my life. You woke up something inside of me. You reminded me that I deserve to be happy. That in this life, we don't get only one shot at a happy ending. There are plenty of chances if we're brave enough to seek them out, and so that's why I'm here. I'm seeking my *new* happy ending. The *right* one, this time. I came here for you, Deja."

"For…me?"

"Yes."

A lone tear rolled down Deja's cheek. She said, "You didn't tell me you were a poet."

He chuckled. "I'm far from it. I'm just telling you what's on my heart and before you commit to anything with me, keep in mind that I come with baggage and plenty of it, but I'm willing to risk it all again if it means I get to be with you."

Deja rose from her seat and wrapped her arms around his neck. Somehow, she also managed to hop out of her seat and land right onto Dare's lap, straddling him. She said, "I don't care what you come with. I'll take you just the way you are." Staring at his lips, she asked, "May I kiss you?"

"You never have to ask me that."

She placed her hands on the sides of his face and kissed him. Delicately. She pulled away, whimpered and kissed him again. Defying the laws of gravity, she floated, drifting to someplace foreign. She'd never been there before. Never felt a potent need tug at her heart. He didn't need to know this was her first time kissing a man. She took her time to savor the moment and brand this experience in her mind for years to come because, unlike Heather, she knew a good man when she saw one, and she was going to hang on to *this* one.

"Deja?"

"Yes?"

"I thought you said you wanted to kiss me?"

She chuckled and sniffled. The tip of her nose danced with his when she responded, "I *did* kiss you."

"Oh." *That's what she thought a kiss was?* He said, "Your kiss was sweet Deja, but I need something deeper."

"Like, how deep?" she asked.

"I can show you better than I can tell you." He quickly captured her mouth before she could utter another word. He didn't go for the safe kiss – he went for it all, sinking his tongue into the recesses of her mouth, then finding her tongue, prompting her to tangle it with his. He heard her whimpers but he kept on, feeding life into the spark she'd put in the center of his chest.

Deja didn't know what to make of him deepening the kiss, but she went with it. When she felt his large, cold hand settle and tighten at the back of her neck, she willingly adjusted and inched forward to accept all he was offering. She was lost for a moment but found herself wedged between him and the steering wheel – bound to him, tasting his lips, his entire mouth while telling herself this man was real. This moment was real.

He'd come here for her. She couldn't be happier.

She pulled away to breathe, but more importantly, to look at him. She wanted to see if what she felt was reciprocated in his light brown eyes. It was – she saw it all. The feeling. The passion. The glimmer of hope that illuminated the path of what they could become.

"Deja Barnett."

"Yes?" she said, her eyes falling to his lips again, tempted to get another taste.

"Will you be my girlfriend?"

"Ahh!" she screamed and fell back. Her butt pressed against the horn, making it go off.

"Deja, you're pressing on the horn.

"Oh, I'm sorry. I got so excited! Oh my gosh," she panted. "This is really happening. Is this happening?"

"Yes, it's happening, and I'm still waiting for an answer. Will you be my girlfriend?"

"I do!" she exclaimed.

He released a deep belly laugh at her answer. "You do?" he asked against her lips. "You realize your answer is sort of not appropriate for my question."

"Is it appropriate and yes, Dare. I do! Over and over and over again, I do," she said, locking her arms around his neck and kissing his lips once more before he again took it a step further.

He released her mouth and said, "I got something for you." He pulled a pink box out of his pocket, opened it and said, "It's a snowflake necklace to always remind you of how we met."

"Aw, Dare, that's so sweet! Thank you."

"You're welcome," he said, hooking the necklace around her neck and then took a small kiss. "I think we should go back inside before they come looking for us."

"No. I think we should stay right here. I want you all to myself."

"We'll have plenty of time for that, sweetheart."

"Okay," she pouted.

Dare pulled the handle to open the door, helping her slide out of his lap, and then he got out behind her.

"So, are we going to tell them?" Deja asked.

"Tell them what?"

"That we're together."

"We probably won't have to. They'll know when I lean over to kiss you."

"You wouldn't kiss me in front of them."

Dare flashed a sneaky grin. "I'll let you think what you want to think."

"Dare…"

Approaching the table, Deja touched her new necklace. Dare pulled out the chair for her and then he took the chair beside her.

Kris asked, "Is everything okay?"

Deja glanced at Kris and then at Sariah's narrowed eyes.

Dare looked at Deja and said, "Yes, everything is fine."

Sariah wasn't buying it. Diverting her attention from Dare to Deja, she asked, "Okay, what's going on with you two?"

"Should I tell them?" Deja leaned over to whisper to Dare.

His eyes crinkled at the corner when he smiled endearingly at her and said, "Have at it."

Deja looked at her sister and said, "Dare and I just got *friend*gaged!"

Tickled, Dare said, "That's the best you could come up with, Deja?"

"What? We're not *en-gaged*. We're *friend*gaged. Get it?"

Dare thought he'd clear up the confusion by saying, "Sariah, I asked your sister to be my girl. She said yes. No, she said, *I do*."

"Woo! That's what I'm talking about!" Kris said, reaching across the table to slap hands with his brother. "Way to get back out there, man. Too bad it had to be *her*."

"Shut up, Kris," Deja told him.

Sariah smiled. She'd had her suspicions about Dare, but the smile on Deja's face told her that her sister knew what she was doing. She looked happy and that made her happy.

"So this is really happening," Sariah said. "Two sisters are marrying two brothers."

"We *just* started dating, Sariah," Deja said. "We're nowhere close to marriage."

"We're not," Dare confirmed. "I want to take time to get to know Deja before we think about taking that leap."

"And there's no rush," Deja said, looking at Dare. She knew what he'd gone through, and she wasn't about to rush him into anything he wasn't ready for.

He leaned in to kiss her like he said he would. Deja held up the menu so Sariah and Kris couldn't see their kissing action.

The waitress came back with the food and said, "Ahem."

Deja pulled back and licked her lips.

"Mmm-hmm…now you're up in here kissing," the waitress said. "Looks like I'll need that butter knife for you and…where'd you find this man?"

Deja laughed. "Do you see that thing sitting right there?" she asked her, pointing to Kris. She said, "This is his brother, Dare. He surprised me with a visit to town, and I can't get enough of him. He's my protector."

"Hi," Dare said to the waitress. "I'm her protector."

The waitress laughed and then asked, "Are you ordering food or—?"

"No," Dare responded. "Their food is already here. I'll snack on these chips."

"Nonsense. You'll share with your *girlfriend*," Deja told him.

Dare's eyes focused on her lips. He couldn't resist the desire to kiss them again, so that's what he did – kiss her and this time, Deja didn't get the chance to hold up a menu. She was too busy focusing on his lips – one, then the other, inside of her mouth and so she moaned and went with it, savoring everything about being this close to him.

Sariah said, "They'll be married in no time."

Kris said, "Yep," and took a bite of the burrito.

CHAPTER 17

DEJA WAS IN the room helping Sariah prep for her big day – the day every girl dreams about – the day of her wedding. Sariah's dress, the dress she had tried on for her, fit perfectly. Her shoes, a pair of golden, sparkly, three-inch heels went perfectly with her gold tiara and earrings. Her makeup was done flawlessly, accentuating her lips and cheekbones. She was stunning.

"You're beautiful, Sariah," Deja said.

"Thank you, Deja. You're looking pretty spiffy yourself."

Deja twirled and said, "Thank you. I hope Dare likes me in gold. He's only seen me in your dress."

"Wait—he was at the fitting?"

"Yes. He showed up briefly to talk to me. I didn't know he would be there."

"Well, don't worry, sis. He'll be blown away when he sees you in this pretty gold dress with your back out looking snatched."

"You think so?"

"I do. You normally dress so drab."

"Oh, I'm so sorry I'm not fashion-forward like you, missy."

"I'll teach you the formula one day, girl. But just know when Dare sees you today…shoot, he may get down on one knee and pop the question."

Deja beamed. "Hey, before I forget, I got you something." Deja walked over to the counter where she'd left her bag. She took out a box and handed it to Sariah.

"Aw, you got me a gift," Sariah said.

"I did."

Sariah opened it and Deja said, "It's a bridal robe."

Sariah held the pink and white lacey robe in front of her and said, "It's beautiful. Thank you, Deja."

"You're welcome."

Sariah embraced her sister. She said, "Thank you for everything. I know I can be a bit extra at times, but I truly appreciate you running all those errands for me."

Deja pulled back and said, "Did you say a bit because that means a little. You're a whole lot of extra and you know it."

Sariah laughed. "I am. I'm sorry but look at it this way. If you hadn't gone up there, you wouldn't have bonded with Dare the way you did."

Deja nodded. "So, I should thank you for

making me taste cakes, try on your dress and check out the venue."

"Absolutely, and if y'all get married, I'm taking the credit for that."

"Of course you are," Deja said, amused.

"I just hope me and Kris will be happy like mom and dad. A lot of marriages don't survive these days."

Their mother, Justine, stepped into the room saying, "Here are my princesses. What's going on?"

"We were talking about how long you and dad have been married and if we thought marriages could last in this day and age."

"Sure, it can," Justine said, "As long as you learn to communicate and forgive each other. You know how you get mad with one of your friends and you stop talking to that person. Well, that won't fly in a marriage. You have to communicate—doesn't matter if you're mad or not."

"How do you do it, Ma?" Sariah asked.

Justine quirked up a brow. "You want the truth? Let me tell you—you pray, honey. You pray and then you pray some mo'."

"That's all?" Deja asked.

"Yes. Pray, and it won't hurt to find a good shot of a lil' *something, something*, too."

"A shot of what, Mama?" Deja asked.

"Something hard and strong, chile. Something that will burn all the way down your esophagus, mess with your mind and make you forget that knucklehead husband of yours ever said or did anything to get on your nerves."

"Mama!" Deja and Sariah said together.

"What? I'm just keepin' it real. You'll find out soon enough, Sariah, and the way Dare be looking at you, Deja, you will, too."

Deja said, "Well, Dare is so handsome, he can get on all of my nerves all he wants."

"You say that now," Justine said.

Sariah said, "Kris already gets on my nerves, so I have a taste of what it'll be like after marriage. I still love him, though."

"That's good, honey, and you are one beautiful bride," Justine said. She hugged Sariah and said, "Mama will always be there for you no matter what. If you need to talk, if you need a break, or if you need a hug—I'll be there."

"I know, Ma. Now, stop it before you make me cry and ruin this whole makeup look."

"Okay, okay. Remember what I said, now."

"I will."

"And you remember it too, Deja, because I'll be having this same talk with you very soon I predict."

"That's what I told her," Sariah said. "Dare is so infatuated."

"He is," Justine said. "Easy on the eyes, too. Both of your men are, but we'll talk about that later. We got to start lining up now before your cousin Carrie loses her mind."

"She's doing a good job keeping everyone in order," Deja said.

"Yes, she is," Justine agreed. "I love you both. See you out there."

"I better get to my position, too," Deja said.

"Alright, sis."

The music began. The packed, well-decorated banquet hall held three hundred guests and all three hundred were due to stay for the reception. The flower girl dropped pink rose petals and then Deja took a few steps forward toward Dare.

Talk about tall, dark and handsome – he was desirable in every way, wrapped up in a neat bow. He looked dapper in the black tuxedo he had on and with the fresh haircut and lineup, not to mention whatever hypnotizing elixir of cologne he'd dabbed on, he was the sexiest, most handsome, mind-blowingly fine man she'd ever laid eyes on.

He took her breath away.

Dare extended his hand to hers. She accepted, feeling his hand close and lock around hers.

"You look absolutely beautiful."

"Thank you, Dare."

As they walked down the aisle, the only thing running through her mind was that this would be her and him one day, taking steps into the realm of forever and Sariah was right – Deja did have her to thank for that. Had she never gone to Shenandoah Valley to fulfill *all* of her sister's many requests, she wouldn't have gotten to know

Dare on the level she had.

When they arrived at the stage, they ascended the stairs. Dare watched her closely as she stepped up, making sure with the tall heels she wore, she navigated every step. When they made it to the stage, instead of releasing her hand, he stood there in front of the minister, prompting her to look at him.

"Dare," she whispered. "I have to go over there. That's what we rehearsed."

"I know," he whispered back.

"Then what are you doing?"

"Taking this all in. This will be us one day."

A smile came to Deja's face. "Think again, buddy. I don't marry men who cheat at hide-n-seek."

Dare smiled, basking in the fact that she always made him do that. Without thinking twice about it, he tilted her chin upward and whispered, "You're absolutely stunning," and then lowered his mouth to hers, kissing her in front of everyone, stirring the guests to cheers. And he didn't stop kissing her when he heard the applause. It only made him kiss her deeper with a hunger he knew he could never satisfy, but didn't mind trying. He kissed her for making him realize there was a second chance for him. His life wasn't over. It was beginning again with Deja – the right woman – whom he'd met in the valley.

I hope you enjoyed reading Dare and Deja's story: *Snowed in at Shenandoah Valley*. Please leave a brief review on Amazon. Want more Deja and Dare? The duo will be featured in four episodes that will be available for purchase initially on my website: www.tinamartin.net!

Episode 1: Reception Romance
Episode 2: Long Distance Troubles
Episode 3: Back to the Valley
Episode 4: Into Forever

After purchasing from the site, you'll have the option of downloading both the **MOBI** file for Kindle and **EPUB** for all other ereaders!

If you prefer to wait to download the books directly from your ebook retailer of choice, they will be offered as a box set titled, **The Dare and Deja Chronicles**. The release date for the box-set is February 11, 2022 and is **available for pre-order now** on Amazon. (You do not have to purchase the box set if you order these books directly from my website.)

SNOWED IN AT *Shenandoah Valley*

Discover other books by Tina Martin:

St. Claire Series
*All books in this series are standalone novels and are full, complete stories. Read them in any order.

Royal
Ramsey
Romulus
Regal
Magnus
Monty
Honeymoon With a St. Claire (A follow-up to Monty)
Major
Just Being Us (A Prequel to Zander)
Zander

Seasons of Love Novelettes
Hot Chocolate: A Winter Novelette
Spring Break: A Spring Novelette

The Boardwalk Bakery Romance
*This is a continuation series that must be read in order.

Baked With Love
Baked With Love 2
Baked With Love 3

The Marriage Chronicles
*This is a continuation series that must be read in order.

Life's A Beach
Falling Out
War, Then Love

The Blackstone Family Series
*All books in this series are standalone novels and are full, complete stories. Read them in any order.

Evenings With Bryson
Leaving Barringer

TINA MARTIN

Forever Us: Barringer and Calista Blackstone (A short story follow-up to *Leaving Barringer*. You must read *Leaving Barringer* before reading this short story)
The Things Everson Lost
Candy's Corporate Crush

A Lennox in Love Series
*All books in this series are standalone novellas and are full, complete stories. Read them in any order.

Claiming You
Making You My Business
Wishing That I Was Yours
Caught in the Storm with a Lennox (A Short Story Prequel to Claiming You)
Before You Say I Do
Winter Wonder
Winter Wedding
The Weekend

Mine By Default Mini-Series:
*This is a continuation series that must be read in order.

Been In Love With You, Book 1
When Hearts Cry, Book 2
You Belong To Me, Book 3
When I Call You Mine, Book 4
Who Do You Love?, Book 5
Forever Mine, Book 6

The Champion Brothers Series:
*All books in this series are standalone novels and are full, complete stories. Read them in any order.

His Paradise Wife
When A Champion Wants You
The Best Thing He Never Knew He Needed
Wives And Champions
The Way Champions Love
His By Spring
A Champion's Proposal

The Accidental Series:
*This is a continuation series that must be read in order.

Accidental Deception, Book 1
Accidental Heartbreak, Book 2
Accidental Lovers, Book 3
What Donovan Wants, Book 4

Dying To Love Her Series:
*This is a continuation series that must be read in order.

Dying To Love Her
Dying To Love Her 2
Dying To Love Her 3

The Alexander Series:
*Books 1-4 must be read in order. Books 5, 6,7 and can be read in any order as a standalone books.

The Millionaire's Arranged Marriage, Book 1
Watch Me Take Your Girl, Book 2
Her Premarital Ex, Book 3
The Object of His Obsession, Book 4
Dilvan's Redemption, Book 5
His Charity Challenge, Book 6 (Heshan Alexander and Charity Eason)
Different Tastes, Book 7 (An Alexander Spin-off novel. Tamera Alexander's Story)
As Long As We Got Love, Book 8 (Family Novel)

Non-Series Titles:
*Individual standalone books that are not part of a series.
Secrets On Lake Drive
Can't Just Be His Friend
The Baby Daddy Interviews
Just Like New to the Next Man
Falling Again
Vacation Interrupted
The Crush
Wasn't Supposed To Love Her

TINA MARTIN

What Wifey Wants
Man of Her Dreams
Bae Watch

ABOUT THE AUTHOR

TINA MARTIN is the author of over 80 romance, romantic suspense and women's fiction titles and has been writing full-time since 2013. Readers praise Tina for her strong heroes, sweet heroines and beautifully crafted stories. When she's not writing, Tina enjoys watching movies, traveling, cooking and spending time with her family.

You can reach Tina by email at **tinamartinbooks@gmail.com** or visit her website for more information at www.tinamartin.net.

Made in the USA
Middletown, DE
02 December 2024

65799829R00130